"What next?" he wondered.

He found out after they had bedded down for the night under the protection of a rock shelf. A hand raised his blanket. He glanced around and saw Andrea slipping in behind him.

He turned to face her. She grabbed his shoulders and pulled him against her. "I need you," she said.

"We'll have to be quiet."

"Why? Let the son of a bitch hear us."

"I was thinking of Blossom."

She laughed. "Yes. But Indian women do not get jealous. And besides, you can have her tomorrow night. I will not protest."

"Nice of you," he said softly . . .

TABOR EVANS

**AND THE
RUNAWAY THIEVES**

A JOVE BOOK

LONGARM AND THE RUNAWAY THIEVES

A Jove Book/published by arrangement with
the author

PRINTING HISTORY
Jove edition/October 1986

ISBN: 0-515-08715-7

Chapter 1

Andrea sat up in the bed and watched Longarm dress. A pleased glow still rested on her lovely features. In the morning's pale light, her dark areolas stood out against her breasts' pale shimmer like dusky roses. She made no effort to cover her nakedness.

Longarm had met her at a poker table the night before. Her dark beauty had immediately attracted him. It soon became obvious to him and the other players that the only reason Andrea had insisted on joining them was Longarm. Once that became clear, Longarm excused himself and cashed in his chips, much to the amusement and relief of the other players. Longarm had been enjoying a series of excellent hands, and so had his new lady friend.

The night that followed had been pleasant but tiring.

"Must you go so soon?" Andrea asked, the slightest trace of a pout on her lush features.

1

"I would've been gone yesterday, but I was too late for the last train north."

"Where are you headed?"

"North Dakota, it looks like."

"That far?"

"I'm lucky. It could have been all the way to Wisconsin."

She slipped lazily down into the bedsheets and patted the empty spot beside her. "You don't have to get dressed right now, do you?"

"The train leaves at ten, Andrea."

"Darling, that means we got plenty of time."

He smiled at her regretfully. "Thanks, but no thanks. You wore me out good and proper last night."

"Are you complaining?"

"On the contrary. I thank you kindly."

"And I thank *you*, mister," she returned, blushing happily at the memory.

Longarm returned his attention to the mirror and finished shaving. He was standing naked in front of his bureau. His shoulders were broad, his shanks lean, and there was not an ounce of spare tallow on his waist. The raw sun and cutting winds of this high country had cured Longarm's face and neck to a saddle-leather brown. His eyes were gunmetal blue, set wide over high cheekbones. Only the tobacco-leaf shade of his close-cropped hair and longhorn mustache gave sure sign of his ancestry. Longarm might easily have passed for a full-blooded Indian, otherwise.

He put his razor down beside the washbasin, dried off his face and neck, then reached for his longjohns. After he pulled them on, he put on his shirt and knotted a dark string tie at his throat. Then he lifted his brown pants off the bed. He had to struggle a bit to get them buttoned. The pants fit snugly because Longarm had deliberately purchased them a size too small. He knew well the dangers of a sweat-soaked fold of cloth or leather between a rider and his mount. The last things he pulled on were his low-heeled cavalry stovepipes. Longarm spent as much time afoot as in the saddle, and in these boots he could run with surprising speed.

"Are you going to leave me here like this?" Andrea asked.

"If you want."

She sighed. "I guess I'll have to get up after all and return to my hotel room."

"If you do, we could have breakfast together in the hotel restaurant."

"That would be nice. Come over here and help me dress."

He grinned down at her. "You know damn well you'd have me undressed in less than a minute."

"Oh, it wouldn't take *that* long, Custis."

Longarm chuckled and slipped on his brown vest, then dropped his double-barreled .44 derringer into its fob pocket, carefully draping across the front of the vest the gold chain clipped to his watch. Then he slung his waxed, heat-hardened cross-draw rig over his left shoulder and shrugged into a brown frock coat that matched his pants. His Colt Model T .44-40 was resting atop his dresser, a pile of cartridges beside it. He dropped the Colt into his shoulder rig, swept the cartridges into his hand, and dropped them into his coat's side pocket.

Andrea smiled mockingly up at him. "Do you think you'll be able to walk, carrying all that hardware?"

"Just don't ask me to bend over. I might not be able to straighten up again." He reached for his hat.

She flung aside the bedsheets. "Aren't you going to wait for me?"

One look at her long-limbed figure and he positioned the snuff-brown Stetson on his head slightly forward, cavalry style, and opened the door.

"I'll wait for you downstairs."

"Coward."

"Yep."

He fled.

Breakfast was over and they were relaxing over coffee. Andrea cleared her throat. "I hate to be a bother, Longarm, but I still have my room just upstairs. We have at least two hours before your train."

"Two hours could not possibly be enough time . . . not for us, anyway."

She blushed. "You are so right, Custis." She sipped her coffee. "Are you allowed to tell me anything about the job Vail is sending you on?"

"There's not much to tell. A bank in Wisconsin was robbed a couple of months ago. The bank robbers took a fortune in silver certificates."

"A fortune? How much?"

Longarm grinned. "Enough to kill for. Enough to finance an armed revolt. The bank in Wisconsin reported an amount close to twenty-five thousand, but banks always overestimate. Billy Vail figures the amount's closer to twenty thousand."

"My God! That much?"

"That is why the local U. S. marshal has already lost three of his best deputies trying to track the thieves. That borderland is pretty rough country, looks like. Before the last deputy died, he managed to get a line on where the fleeing bank robbers went. Apparently they fled into Canada, passing through a town called Moosehead in North Dakota."

"So now it's a Canadian problem."

"Technically. Their mounted police have been battling U. S. whiskey smugglers in that region for years. That's why they were brought in to begin with. But there's still too much smuggling going on, and the Canadian authorities have asked our government for help."

"They have?"

"Yes. This bank robber is also a whiskey smuggler, they believe. Billy Vail has assured me that if I go into Canada after him, I can expect the full cooperation of the Canadian government. And they would not block me from taking him back to the States for trial."

"You get him for trial and the Canadian government gets rid of a troublemaker. Is that it?"

"That's it." Longarm nodded.

"And for that you must ride all the way to Moosehead?"

Longarm nodded unhappily. He was not looking forward to the journey at all.

"I am tired of talking about the case. Sometimes I think men are just little boys, running around shooting each other with their shiny guns."

"You might have a point there."

Andrea glanced at the grandfather clock in the corner. Then she leaned forward and smiled wickedly. "I'm not going to ask you again," she said softly. "But I imagine that train ride is going to be a hot, miserable ride. Don't you think?"

"It will be all of that."

She smiled and got to her feet. "Then why not have something pleasant to think back on? My room number is 413." She turned and walked into the hotel lobby, heading for the wide marble stairs beyond the front desk.

Longarm dug into his frock-coat pocket for some money to pay the check. Room 413, was it? Well, maybe two hours would give the two of them enough time for a proper goodbye, at that.

Even for an improper goodbye.

During the long train ride, which was just as tiresome and as miserable as Andrea had predicted, Longarm studied the dossier Vail had given him on the presumed leader of the bank robbers. Rene Dupre was a Metis, a Canadian of French and Indian extraction, known to the Canadian authorities as one of the most active and resourceful of the Metis leaders.

The Canadian authorities were convinced that the money Dupre had stolen from the Wisconsin bank was to be used by his fellow Metis to finance their activities. Yet if the authorities were to lay a hand on Dupre, it would arouse the ire of his explosive followers and simply precipitate the very revolt Gabriel Roubison and other Metis leaders seemed anxious to bring about.

The Canadian government's great fear was that the Metis might succeed in a revolt that would establish a state of their own and cut the rest of Canada off from its western provinces. The most powerful Metis leader was Louis Riel. Earlier, before fleeing to exile in Montana, Riel had almost succeeded in establishing his own independent Metis state. If another Metis revolt became established, Riel would most assuredly return to Canada to lead it. A fiery, powerful orator, his return at the head of a well-financed Metis force could cause considerable trouble.

As Vail had explained to him, the hope was that Longarm would capture Dupre and bring him back to the United States above the "protests" of the Canadian government. The Metis would then have no one to blame but a federal

6

U. S. marshal and the foreign government that employed him. And Dupre would leave Canada, not as a brave leader fighting for his people, but as a common criminal, a bank robber. It was a cynical deal, perhaps, but one that had advantages for both countries.

Unfortunately, the dossier Vail had given Longarm contained no picture or sketch of Rene Dupre. All Longarm had to go on was a general description of the Metis. On the other gang members, there was little or no information at all.

With a weary sigh, Longarm put aside the dossier and looked out the coach window at the bleak landscape. Soon he would be passing the Pembina River, a few miles from Moosehead. There he was to meet with an officer of the Northwest Mounted Police, a man whose code name was MacIver. MacIver was to help Longarm mix in with the whiskey smugglers and cross unofficially into Canada. He and Longarm were to infiltrate the smugglers in order to get a line on Dupre.

Longarm was not so sure he liked the idea. He had always worked alone, and preferred the freedom of operation it allowed him.

He turned his head away from the window and rested his head back. This was likely to be a long and difficult mission. Apprehending bank robbers was one thing. Tangling with politically motivated zealots was something else again.

The moment the desk clerk heard Longarm ask for Mr. MacIver's room, he began to sweat. Tiny beads of perspiration stood out on his upper lip. The fellow wore red silk sleeve garters, and the polished dome under his thinning hair reflected the light from the lobby's single chandelier.

"Mr. MacIver, did you say?"

"I did. Anything wrong?" Longarm placed his bag down on the counter.

"Of course not. Now, let's see. That would be Room 34. Right up those stairs, sir."

Instructing the desk clerk to keep an eye on his bag, Longarm strode across the lobby and up the stairs. Room 34 was at the end of a narrow hallway. He knocked. There was no response. He knocked again. This time a voice called out, telling him to come in. Longarm did not like that. The man should have been a little more careful, at least ask who it was. Recalling the nervous desk clerk, he drew his Colt.

"You in there, Sammy?" he called through the door, his voice a high falsetto.

Longarm heard a muttered oath, the sound of a chair scraping, and then the tread of heavy boots approaching the door. As soon as it was open a crack, Longarm lowered his shoulder and charged into the room. The fellow at the door was sent reeling back against the wall. Another man was standing in a corner behind the bed, and a third was crouched by the window.

Longarm dove for the floor as the two men blasted at him with their sixguns. Hot lead slammed into the floor, following after Longarm as he rolled under the bed. He came out on the other side of it, firing up at the man crouching behind it. This one developed a sudden leak in his gut and collapsed forward onto the mattress.

Coming all the way up from behind the bed, Longarm shot twice at the gunman in the corner. He was hit, but managed to fling himself out through the window, taking most of the sash with him. Longarm heard him strike the porch roof below and turned his attention to the one who had opened the door. This gunman was already ducking out

8

the door, flinging a wild shot back at Longarm as he did so.

Longarm vaulted over the bed and chased after him down the narrow hallway. An old man, tying his bathrobe, stepped out of his room to check on all the commotion and was knocked flat by the fleeing gunman. Longarm leaped over his sprawled body in time to see his quarry plunge down a narrow flight of back stairs.

When he reached the ground floor, Longarm heard the sudden pound of hoofs. Bursting out into the alley, he caught sight of the fleeing horseman. He had time for one shot. He strode out into the center of the alley. Spreading his feet, he steadied himself, aimed at the base of the horse's tail, and fired.

Longarm was lucky. His round carried high. The rider caught the .44 slug squarely in his back and peeled off his horse. Longarm watched him hit. The fellow rolled over slowly, crawled a few feet farther on, then collapsed face down.

Longarm turned and ran back into the hotel. He was up the stairs in four or five giant strides. The old man was just getting up off the floor. Longarm was unable to leap over him, and the two went down in a tangle of arms and legs. Mumbling an apology, Longarm leapt to his feet and rushed back to MacIver's room.

The hallway was filling up with eager, excited spectators. Longarm pushed through them and slammed the door in their faces. The gunman he had shot in the gut was still lying face down on the bedspread, a pool of blood spreading under him. Longarm flung the man over. No help there. He was dead.

Where was MacIver?

Longarm noticed that the closet door was slightly ajar. He walked over and flung it all the way open. The man he assumed was Ian MacIver was hanging on a hook stuck through his collar, his head sagging to one side. His skull had been smashed in brutally. Blood had poured from the wound, covering most of his vest and shirtfront, and was still slowly dripping in a black, congealing stain at his feet.

Someone was pounding on the room's door. Longarm ignored it and walked over to the window and looked out through the shattered glass. The man who had flung himself onto the porch roof was still there, sprawled face down, his hand clutching his revolver.

A key clashed into the lock and the door swung open. Longarm turned. The sheriff pushed his way into the room. He was a big, beefy fellow with a sandy handlebar mustache and a belly that sagged out over his gunbelt. In his large, meaty hand he held a gleaming Navy Colt. Behind him, the near-solid crush of onlookers crowded in closer, staring with horrid fascination at the body lying on the bed. The desk clerk was in the nearest rank, the key he had just used still in his hand. An agitated older man who looked to be the hotel manager stood at his side.

"What the hell's goin' on here?" the sheriff demanded.

"Close the door and I'll tell you."

"Put down your gun first!"

"God damn it, Sheriff, I said close that door!"

When the sheriff saw the look in the big lawman's eyes, he turned and shut the door.

"You got a name, Sheriff?"

"Jud Bullock, and I'm still tellin' you to put that shootin' iron away."

Longarm dropped the .44 into his cross-draw rig. "Look out the window, Sheriff."

The sheriff lumbered over to the window and glanced down. When he saw the dead, spread-eagled gunman on the porch roof, he swore. He pulled his head back in and looked in some astonishment at Longarm. "You shot that one, too?"

"I did. The son of a bitch was in here with that one on the bed, waiting to bushwhack me."

The sheriff walked past Longarm and peered at the man on the bed. He went slightly pale. "You killed this one, too?"

"That's right."

"There's a dead man in the alley out back of the hotel. What do you know about him?"

"He was the third son of a bitch."

"You mean you killed all three?" the sheriff asked.

"Unless you've got a better explanation."

"Why?"

"I told you. They were in this room, trying to bushwhack me."

"This is your room?"

"Nope."

"Then how did they know you'd be in here?" the local lawman asked.

"Look in the closet, Sheriff."

The big man walked nervously over to the closet. Longarm had closed the closet door. The sheriff pulled it open. There was just enough light for him to see MacIver.

"Jesus," the sheriff said softly.

"Call the desk clerk in here," Longarm suggested. "He let those three in here so they could bushwhack me."

"How the hell do you know that?"

"Just do as I say, will you, Sheriff? Or I'll figure you're in on this with him."

The man's round face went beet red, but he managed to control himself and pull open the door. "Elmer!" he said to the desk clerk. "Get in here!"

Elmer edged unhappily into the room. The sheriff

closed the door behind him. The desk clerk looked nervously at Longarm.

"Mr. MacIver's dead, Elmer," Longarm told him.

"My God!"

"Elmer, you knew those three men were up here waiting for me, didn't you?"

The desk clerk swallowed, his Adam's apple bobbing frantically. He pulled at his collar. "Yes, sir," he said. "I did."

"Why didn't you tell me?"

"They said if I let on, they'd come back down and blow me from here to hell and back."

"So you told no one, waited until I showed, and then let me walk up here into a trap."

"I didn't know it was a trap, exactly."

"What did you think it was? A party?"

He shook his head miserably.

"Damn it, Elmer. Why didn't you warn me, or at least tell the sheriff?"

The desk clerk was trembling. "I was . . . scared, sir. They were very . . . frightening men."

"All right. Settle down. Who were they? Metis?"

Elmer nodded, perspiration standing out on his bald pate.

"You ever seen them before tonight?"

"No, sir."

"Strangers in town, were they?"

"I . . . think so."

"Get out of here."

Elmer turned and fled the room. Longarm turned to the sheriff. "There's more Metis where those three came from, Sheriff. And they won't be far." Indicating the dead man on the bed, Longarm asked, "You seen that one over there before?"

The sheriff peered unhappily at the riddled body. "No," he replied. "We got no breeds in this town. These Metis must've come from across the river. Canada ain't that far, and it's easy enough to slip back and forth across the border."

"You are absolutely sure you haven't seen that dead man before?"

"I just told you, didn't I? And right now this town's got to bury four dead men and you still ain't given me no proper explanation."

"I came up here to meet that poor son of a bitch hanging in the closet, Sheriff," Longarm said. "These men evidently knew I'd be coming up here to meet him and were waiting for me."

"Why in hell would them three want to bushwhack you, mister? What's your game, anyway?"

Longarm shrugged. "No game, Sheriff. Like I just said, we had some business to conduct in the quiet of your little hamlet."

The sheriff looked uneasily at Longarm. "What kind of business?"

"You don't need to know that, Sheriff."

"God damn it! You can't come in here and kill three people, then refuse to tell me what you're doin' here! I got a right to know!"

"All you've got a right to do is keep the peace around here. From the looks of things, you ain't doing a very good job. But I'm not a man to hold a grudge, Sheriff."

"Yeah? Well, at least you can tell me who this MacIver is. What's *his* business?"

Longarm knew what MacIver was supposed to be and saw no reason for keeping it from the sheriff. "I believe he's a whiskey drummer, Sheriff."

The sheriff's eyes opened wider. A light was dawning

13

in his brain, sending a feeble glow over a vast darkness. "And that's what you are, too! You're a whiskey drummer, too, ain't you?"

"Now that would be telling."

"I thought so! Listen, mister. We got enough smugglers in this county. All you fellows do is cause trouble. So I'm tellin' you, mister. Pack your goods and take the first train out of town."

Longarm shrugged and looked over at the man on the bed. "I guess I have no choice," he said. "Looks like whiskey drummers ain't so welcome in this town."

"You guessed right, mister."

"I'll stay the night if you don't mind, Sheriff, then leave in the morning."

"Just so I don't see you around here after that train pulls out."

Longarm nodded abruptly, opened the room's door, and pushed out into the hallway through the crowd of onlookers. The desk clerk was gone. Longarm descended the stairs to the lobby and found the clerk back at his post. When the fellow saw Longarm approaching, he took out a handkerchief and began to mop his brow.

"I'll want a room for the night," Longarm told him, lifting his alligator bag off the desk top. "At the rear and on the third floor. Do you have one vacant up there?"

"Yes, sir."

Longarm signed the register as John T. Blake. It was the alias he and Billy Vail had settled on. Then he went up to his room to get ready for his next move.

His day wasn't over yet.

Chapter 2

Lying fully clothed on his bed, Longarm stirred. It was night at last. His room was in the back of the hotel, but he could still hear faintly the increase in horse traffic, the steady burst of revelry from the saloons, a door slamming every now and then, and, like a steady, sad accompaniment to all the supposed merriment, the hectic laughter of the women of the night.

He got up off the bed and checked his Colt. Then he opened the window, turned around, and sat on the sill. The roof had no gutter. He had checked on that earlier. Reaching up, he grabbed the edge of the roof with both hands and pulled himself up onto the roof. Perched there in the darkness, he felt slightly ridiculous as he peered back down into his room. If any uninvited guests broke in on him, they would find an empty room for their trouble—and make an excellent target for Longarm.

He had decided against telegraphing Vail, though Vail

had insisted he keep in touch if anything went awry. Telegraphers could be the biggest gossips in town, and there was a chance the one in this town would not wait long before he let it slip that the new stranger in town, the one who just shot three Metis, had just sent a wire to Marshal Billy Vail in Denver.

Longarm was on his own now, way out on a limb—or was it a roof—with half the limb cut off. MacIver was to have helped him make contact with one of the many gangs smuggling whiskey across the border. Since the Metis were also smuggling whiskey to gain funds for their organization, Vail had directed Longarm to get into the business himself in order to meet up with Dupre's gang. It had been a long shot from the very beginning, and it looked a hell of a lot longer now. Someone had sent word what was afoot. Whether the informer was in Canada or in Denver was anyone's guess. But there was no question those three Metis had been waiting for him—and for poor MacIver, as well. Longarm's only hope now was that despite MacIver's death he would still be able to contact members of a whiskey smuggling gang.

Darkness came. The sound of revelry in the town below slowly tapered off. Around eleven o'clock it petered out almost completely. A little after twelve the door to Longarm's room opened just a crack. Peering over the edge of the roof, Longarm waited. A short, powerful figure entered, gun in hand. Cautiously he approached Longarm's bed. Behind him entered two, then three more men. Each man had drawn his revolver.

The first man looked over at the open window. Longarm ducked back. He heard the intruder walk over to the window and look out. The man spoke in a bastard French to his friends, then slammed the window down. A moment later the door was pulled shut behind the four men as they left Longarm's room.

Longarm sat back on the roof, a pleased smile on his face. When the first intruder had looked around the room, Longarm had been able to get a pretty good look at his swarthy, hawk-like face. Longarm would never forget that glance or the cold, steely glint of the man's dark eyes. If this man was a Metis—and Longarm was certain he was —then Longarm might well have been looking into the face of the man he had come so far to apprehend, Rene Dupre.

Longarm waited a decent interval, then moved back along the roof. He dropped lightly to the roof of the back porch, then down to the alley floor. Moving up the alley alongside the hotel, he was in time to see the four intruders mount up and ride out. Longarm crossed the street quickly to the livery and rented a black, paying dearly for his inability to dicker. A few minutes after the Metis left town, Longarm took out after them.

He drew in sight of them as they dismounted on a flat beside the Pembina River's shore, close to where it entered Canada. Pulling up, Longarm dismounted and moved through the sparse timber until he was close enough to see what the four men were up to. The moon was high in a cloudless sky and he could see them clearly.

A barge-like riverboat was being poled across the river toward the waiting men. When the flat boat got close enough, the four men splashed into the water to drag its bow up onto the sandy shore. One of the men disappeared into the timber and returned driving a high-sided wagon piled high with whiskey barrels—or what passed for whiskey. Two powerful work horses were pulling it and they had to labor mightily to haul the loaded wagon over the soft ground. The men clambered up into the wagon and began transferring the barrels and casks to the flat boat.

Longarm slipped through the timber until he was between the men and the shore. They worked quickly, silently, loading the boat. A ramp had been thrown down from the boat and the men were using two-wheeled carts, grunting as they hauled the precious cargo onto the boat. The man Longarm was almost certain was Dupre stood on the flat boat barking orders to the others, the sharp edge of his voice cutting cleanly through the cool night.

What happened next was never very clear to Longarm.

Two men ran out of the timber close to the spot where Longarm had tethered his horse. They had guns in their hands and were screaming curses at the men loading the flat boat. Another man ran out of the woods only a few feet from Longarm. The Metis clawed for their sixguns. The night exploded with the bark of gunfire. Flame spat from muzzles. Men cried out, fell. Two were grappling waist-deep in the water. At once the leader of the Metis began poling frantically away from the shore.

More men rushed from the woods. One of them splashed into the water, then clawed his way onto the boat. He should have saved his energy. Dupre dropped the pole and shot him in the gut, then kicked him in the head, sending him overboard. The fellow splashed weakly, then gave up. He uttered a tiny cry and let the current take him. By this time, Dupre was at midstream. He kept on poling, and did not look back. In a moment he was swept out of sight down the river.

Longarm ducked lower and began to pull back away from the fighting men. Stray shots were shearing the branches above his head. His foot stepped into the shallows. He lost his balance and his back slapped the water loudly as he hit. Two of the attacking men, alerted by the sound, hurried over, their sixguns out, their blood-lust aroused. In a moment they were looming over Longarm, their faces savage as they contemplated their victim.

Longarm clawed for his gun, but he was only able to get off one shot before a round from the closest one caught him in the thigh. He turned and flung himself into the water. The fellow who had shot him waded out after him and grabbed hold of the skirt of Longarm's frock coat, ripping open the side pocket. Longarm felt his wallet and most of his folding money and silver slipping into the swirling waters. But there was nothing he could do about it as he swung around in the hip-deep water and belted the man in the jaw. Staggered, the man stepped back some, shaking his head to clear it. Longarm didn't wait for it to get clear. He caught the edge of the fellow's chin with a brutal punch that sent him spinning.

As the man collapsed face down in the swift water, Longarm flung himself out into the stream and began to pull for the far shore. The second of the two men, standing in the shallows, began firing at him, the rounds sending up short geysers of water all around him. Longarm ducked his head under the water and kept swimming. The sound of the bullets spanking the water came to him as a curious, bell-like sound. Surfacing farther out, he continued to pull hard for the distant shore. One round ricocheted off the water and nicked him in the shoulder. It felt like a bee sting, nothing worse.

He looked back at the shore. The attackers seemed to have given up on him and were busy shooting the two dray horses. A moment later they vanished into the timber along the shore, leaving behind a litter of bodies along the river-bank.

The current took hold of him. Soon it was pulling him

roughly downstream. He tried to fight it, but he no longer had the strength. A steady stream of blood was pulsing out of his thigh. He put his head down and let the current carry him, stroking just enough to stay on the surface. He was pulled around a long meander, the swift current eventually pulling him toward the Canadian shore.

As he swept closer to the dark embankment, he saw just ahead of him a tree leaning far out over the water. Most of its base had been swept away and it lay directly across his path, barely inches above the swift water. Longarm ducked, but not soon enough. The tree cracked him hard on the side of his head. Gasping, he tried to keep afloat. His heavy, booted feet dragged him down. He felt himself twisting in the current. The hard clammy surface of a submerged rock slammed into him. For a moment he thought the blow might have broken his shoulder. He clung to the rock, his senses reeling, then pulled himself up onto it until his head broke the surface. The boulder was only a few feet from the riverbank.

As soon as he could manage it, he struggled the remaining distance to the embankment. He was now in Canada, he realized, but this fact had little importance to him now. He had to see to his wound or he would bleed to death.

But he was too weak to do anything about it before he collapsed face down onto a stretch of cool grass and passed out.

"Get up, mister! Get up!"

Longarm opened his eyes. A boy of about twelve was bent over him. He had one hand under Longarm's arm and was trying to pull him erect.

"You can't stay here!" the boy cried in a rough French accent that made it difficult for Longarm to understand him. "You'll bleed to death!"

Longarm shook his head. "Can't get up," Longarm muttered. "Get help."

The boy turned and disappeared into the night. Longarm looked down at his thigh. It was bleeding a lot more slowly now, but this gave him little comfort. It just meant there was less blood for him to lose now.

He crawled over to a willow, grabbed the trunk, and pulled himself to a sitting position. He threw off his jacket, ripped his shirt into strips, and wound it as tight as he could manage around the bleeding thigh. He used the barrel of his .44 to tighten the bandage until the bleeding finally ceased. He realized he could lose his leg if he kept the tourniquet this tight for very long, but it was a chance he was willing to take.

He heard the brush stir beside him, turned, and saw a wounded man emerge from the woods. He had a bloody bandage wound around his waist. With him was Sheriff Bullock. The sheriff smiled when he saw Longarm.

"Well, well, well," he said. "Look what we got here." He bent and removed the Colt from Longarm's bandage and tossed it into the brush.

Straightening, he grinned down at Longarm. He had not forgotten Longarm's insolent manner when the two had met earlier. It still rankled. Now he was about to set matters straight.

"I knew you'd turn up with that gang of half-breeds," he told the lawman. "This here's our border crossin'. We been usin' it since seventy-eight an' we ain't givin' it up for no damned breeds. You tied in with the wrong outfit, mister." He grinned. "So I guess maybe you can forget that train ride. You're goin' on a different ride, an' when you finish, your ass'll be fryin' in hell!"

"Well, I'll just save some of that fried ass for you, Sheriff."

"Yeah, you do that, mister."

The sheriff cocked his gun and stepped closer. Longarm's apparent helplessness was an irresistible lure. He kicked Longarm in the side and smiled when he saw Longarm's involuntary grimace of pain. Bullock could not resist kicking Longarm a second time, harder. Then he bent closer and examined the gold washed chain hanging across Longarm's soaked vest, between his watch and his fob pocket. The sheriff's small, greedy eyes lit up. He reached out for the watch.

Longarm said, "Hell, Sheriff. You don't want this watch. The water must've ruined it."

The sheriff slapped Longarm, a mean backhand that caused his teeth to rattle. "Shut up. No one tells me what I need."

Bullock pulled the watch out of Longarm's vest pocket. Resigned, it seemed, to helping him, Longarm lifted the watch fob out of his vest pocket with his right hand. His eyes still on the watch, Bullock did not see the derringer's gleam as Longarm palmed it—then cocked and fired both barrels.

Only one chamber fired, but it was enough to send a slug into Bullock's gut just below his sagging belt. Gasping, Bullock dropped his Colt and the watch. He clutched at his shattered stomach with both hands and staggered back, eyes wide in terror. He knew at once that the wound was fatal.

The other man was too stupid to fling his hands into the air. Instead, he slapped leather hastily in an attempt to draw his holstered weapon. Longarm snatched up the sheriff's revolver and pulled the trigger. The big weapon leaped in his hand. The round crashed into the man's chest, squarely over the heart.

Both men sagged to the ground, their life's blood ebbing away.

Watching them, Longarm wondered how he was going to prevent himself from trooping into hell right after them. The moment Bullock tossed away Longarm's gun and loosened the tourniquet, his thigh wound had opened up again. By this time he was beginning to feel lightheaded, and he was about to lose consciousness when the darkness behind him came alive with running feet.

The boy who had left him earlier reappeared. Behind him came a young girl of eighteen or nineteen, her white nightdress billowing as she ran. Not until the two reached the clearing did they see the sheriff and his companion on the grass. In the moon's cold light, the two men looked like enormous, slowing twisting worms.

The boy and the girl pulled up, eyes wide.

"He's killed them," the boy said, his voice hushed.

"Sorry about these two," Longarm managed. "They were about to finish me off. I had no choice."

"Guess you didn't at that, mister!" the boy said. "Sheriff Bullock was a real mean son of a bitch. This was his deputy, Tate. You sure fixed their wagon."

"I'm not out of the woods yet myself, boy," Longarm said, indicating his thigh wound. "There's a bullet in there needs to come out."

The girl brushed past the boy and knelt beside Longarm. Pulling away the bandage, she peered at the wound. Then she looked at the boy. "Go back and get the flatbed, Tim!" she told him, her French accent somewhat easier to understand than the boy's.

Tim disappeared back the way he had come. It seemed to Longarm that all he saw of the boy was his flying heels. Smiling to hide her concern, the girl looked back at Longarm.

23

"My name is Sharon," she told him. "Once I get you home, I'll take that bullet out."

"You think you can do that?"

"For many years I live close to this border. I been gettin' very used to poking for bullets."

"Whiskey smugglers?"

She nodded briskly. "Them and the liquored-up Indians. Ain't a very pleasant combination."

"I can imagine."

"I don't really think you can," she said.

"I stand corrected."

She blushed. "I am so sorry. I didn't mean to sound impertinent."

"You sounded just fine."

"How does she feel? The wound, I mean."

"Hurts like hell." He looked beyond her at the two dead men on the grass behind her. "I guess it don't hurt them much any more."

"Good riddance," she snapped. "Them two were leading the biggest gang of whiskey runners this side of Pembina. You a lawman?"

Longarm was startled. "What made you ask that?"

"Just wondered. It's about time the law caught up with them two and the rest of their gang."

Longarm decided then that he would forget the alias he and Vail had settled on. If there had been an informant, the name they had chosen would be a dead giveaway to anyone in the Meti camp. "Name's Ned," Longarm told her. "Ned Barker. I'm just a drifter, lookin' for work and maybe a ranch that needs a top hand."

"How'd you get mixed up in this?"

"I was headin' for Moosehead, heard some shootin', and got off my horse to see what all the commotion was. Looks like I found out."

24

She frowned at the wound in his thigh. "Curiosity killed the cat," she reminded him.

"And it's damn near killed me."

"It won't," she promised him. She looked past Longarm in the direction the boy Tim had taken.

A second later, Longarm heard the sound of a wagon rattling over rough ground. Longarm grabbed the tree trunk and pulled himself upright. A rocking dizziness assailed him and he almost pitched forward. The girl moved quickly closer and braced him against the tree.

The wagon pulled up alongside. The boy jumped down and with his sister's help managed to get Longarm up into the bed of the wagon. The exertion caused Longarm's head to spin. He propped himself up against the side of the wagon and called out to Tim.

The boy was in the act of climbing up onto the seat. "What is it, mister?"

"My gun," Longarm told him. "It's over there, near the bushes."

After a quick search Tim plucked Longarm's big .44 out of the grass. He handed it to Longarm, then climbed up onto the wagon's seat. Crouching beside Longarm in the bed of the wagon, Sharon urged her brother to hurry. Tim snapped his whip and shouted at the team.

The wagon lurched forward. Longarm felt himself slipping to one side. Sharon moved over beside him and pulled him down so that his head rested in her lap. The last thing he remembered before he passed out was her cool hand on his brow.

Chapter 3

In the week that followed, while Longarm tossed fever-ishly between darkness and light, the countryside around the shacks where Sharon and her brother Tim lived re-sounded with the pounding of horses' hoofs as posses and mean-eyed horsemen searched for sign of the sheriff's killer.

Twice, on the sudden approach of riders, Longarm had been hastily carried to a hidden root cellar at the rear of the house. Once he had been conscious enough to hear the rough voices of the men questioning Sharon, and her clear, sharp responses as she assured the men that no murdering whiskey drummer had been seen near their place.

As Longarm learned later, the sensational death of Sheriff Bullock and his deputy, as well as the slaughter of the smugglers on the American side of the river, had been carried by newspapers as far south as Bismarck. Soon thereafter the Eastern papers picked up the story, and before they were through with it, the gunfight had turned into border warfare. It was weeks before the story faded from the front pages. No one, of course, made any mention of the fact that until his death Sheriff Bullock had undoubtedly been the leader of a rival gang of smugglers, the most active along the Canadian border.

Longarm turned his head. "Sharon?"

She looked back quickly. "Oh! You startled me," she said. She had been stealing quietly from the room after parting the curtains. A solid beam of sunlight, alive with gleaming dust motes, had planted itself on the foot of his bed. She peered anxiously at him. "How do you feel?"

"Much better, thanks. My fever broke early this morning."

"You must be hungry."

"Yes," he said.

"I have some broth on the stove," she told him, and vanished out the door. She returned almost at once with a steaming bowl of broth, which she put down on the nightstand next to his bed. Longarm sat up and put his feet down on the floor. For a moment he felt dizzy, but that did not last.

Then he set to work filling the sudden, enormous cavern under his ribs. When he finished his third bowl of broth, two thick slices of fresh bread, and a cup of hot coffee, he thanked her and asked where Tim was.

She took away the napkin she had tucked under his chin. "Tim's gone to pick apples," she told him. "He thinks there might be some we can use in an abandoned orchard below the stream."

"I heard his voice in the kitchen this morning. He was wondering if I was ever going to wake up."

She smiled. "You have been unconscious for some time."

"If Tim hadn't come along when he did, I'd be a dead man now—or rotting in a jail cell. I'd like to thank him."

"He was very proud he could help you, especially when he saw what you did to Sheriff Bullock."

"That wasn't a pretty sight for a boy his age. How old is he?"

"Twelve. He's seen much worse, Ned."

"What was he doing at the river that late?"

"He heard the shooting. He thought our brother might have been part of it. Justin has been smuggling whiskey lately, I am afraid."

"An older brother?"

"Yes."

"He's not living here?"

"No. He's living near Crystal City with his woman. It is no longer safe around here for him. He is wanted by the Mounted Police, supposedly for plotting revolution against Ottawa. But that is nonsense. All Justin does is drink and play cards with his cronies. They talk a lot, but do nothing."

"You sound disappointed," Longarm said.

She shrugged.

"I'd like to get up now," he went on.

"Do you think you should?"

He nodded and smiled. "Yes. And I would also like to take a bath."

She stood up, smiling. "I'll bring in the tub, then heat the water."

Half an hour later, as Longarm stepped into the steaming tub, Sharon brought in his washed underdrawers and shirt, along with his cleaned and pressed trousers, his frock coat

29

and vest. Placing them down on the bed, she put down his stovepipes alongside the tub. The boots, Longarm noticed, had been polished to a gleaming finish.

She looked down at his long, rawboned figure sitting in the steaming water. "You need a shave."

She left the room and returned a moment later with a straight razor, a shaving brush, and a mug. Unbuttoning her dress at the neck and rolling up her sleeves, she knelt by the tub and proceeded to lather his face.

"Don't be nervous," she told him, leaning close, her warm breath like a perfume. "I used to shave my brother all the time, and he never complained."

"It's not that razor i'm afraid of," he told her.

"Oh?" she said, smiling slightly.

She worked swiftly and deftly. When she finished, she brought in a steaming bucket of water and emptied it unceremoniously over his head. The water was so hot he grabbed the sides of the tub to prevent himself from leaping out of it.

With the steam still billowing up about him, she began soaping his thick hair. Stinging suds flowed down over his forehead and into the corners of his eyes. He grimaced as her strong fingers massaged his scalp. Without warning, she pulled him forward, then shoved his head down into the steaming water. He tried to straighten up. She pushed his head down farther. When she did allow him up, he was blowing like a seal.

She emptied another bucket of near-scalding water over him. Gasping, he fought for breath and heard her mischievous laughter. He squinted at her.

"You trying to drown me?"

"Poor dear," she said, her eyes dancing, no hint of remorse in them.

She took up the soap and sponge and scrubbed his back.

Then she worked on his shoulders, arms, and the front of his chest. He felt his pores steaming open and relished each stroke of her sponge. Closing his eyes, he leaned back and relaxed, almost falling asleep under her soothing ministrations.

He felt her perfumed breath on his face as she suddenly leaned closer. He opened his eyes to look at her. She smiled, her teeth flashing brilliantly in her dusky face.

"You have a very fine body," she said. "There is no fat. It is hard, like a healthy cat."

"I wouldn't know about cats," he said.

She laughed softly as she continued to scrub his heavily muscled chest and shoulders. Her plunging hand moved still farther down the front of his chest, well past the thick mat of short, curly hair.

"Mmm," she said, as she stroked deep into his crotch.

Her fingers did not flinch away from what they found there. She glanced at him and smiled, destroying what little composure he had left. But before he could pull her to him, she released him and stood up. With the back of her hand, she brushed a stray lock of hair off her damp forehead.

"Stand up," she said.

Longarm pushed himself to his full height. Her dark eyes flashed mischievously, but she did not embarrass him by commenting with either word or glance on his erection as she busied herself scrubbing the small of his back, his tight, solid buttocks, and finally the back of his legs. She was very thorough, and with each passing second, Longarm grew more rigid.

Two more steaming buckets of hot water rinsed him off, but did little to ease the urgency of his condition. Then she folded a huge towel about his waist and helped him out of the tub. She patted him dry then, her hands playing a maddening tune over his tingling body. She draped a second towel over his dripping face and head and rubbed his hair dry. Finished, she stepped back, leaving the towel still draped over his face. He heard the door close and yanked off the towel.

She was gone.

The next day Longarm was sitting outside in the shade of a large ponderosa when a hard-riding bunch approached the house so fast it was impossible for him to hide. Sharon ran out with her rifle. Tim stayed in the house, standing at the nearest window, a shotgun in his hand.

"Who're these riders?" Longarm asked.

"English," she said bitterly. "English Canadians."

"You know them?"

She nodded. "That's John Masters riding in front. Those are his militia. At least, that's what the English call them."

"What are they after?"

"They want to clear this land of our kind."

"Your kind?"

She looked at him, surprised he didn't already know. "Metis," she told him.

"I thought maybe you were," he told her. "Just wanted to make sure."

The horsemen pulled to a halt in front of Longarm. Bits jingled and leather squeaked. Dust billowed up and hung in the hot afternoon air. The riders chucked their hats back and rested their hands on their saddlehorns.

John Masters nudged his horse closer until he towered over Sharon and Longarm. Masters was a lean, red-haired fellow with a lantern jaw. His green eyes were lit now with powerful indignation. Though it was considered poor manners to remain in the saddle when addressing your betters or your equals, Masters remained on his horse.

Sharon stepped back deliberately and raised her rifle,

the muzzle pointed at Masters's face. He did not blink or pay her much mind. Instead, he turned his head to address Longarm.

"Who're you, mister?"

"Name's Ned," Longarm said, cheerfully enough. "Ned Barker. Who're you?"

He ignored Longarm's question. "What are you doin' here?"

"Just riding through."

"Saddle tramp, eh?"

Longarm shrugged.

"You'd be wise to keep on ridin'." Masters turned his attention to Sharon. "You're still on this land, I see. I thought I told you and your brother to get off it."

"We ain't gettin' off, Mr. Masters. Justin told me to stay put, and that's just what we're doin'."

"Where is the son of a bitch?"

She tossed her head angrily, but kept her temper. "My *brother* is not here. If he were, you wouldn't be ridin' in so bold."

He snorted. "So it may please you to think." Masters looked back at Longarm. "Like I said, mister, keep on ridin'. Get out of this. It ain't none of your concern. Stay here and you'll be part of it soon enough."

"Part of what, Mr. Masters?"

"This here rebellion, that's what."

Longarm shrugged. "I don't see any rebellion."

Masters looked back at Sharon. "I'm givin' you till midnight to clear out!" he told her.

Then he hauled his horse back cruelly. The animal, a fine powerful chestnut, fought the bit and shook his head angrily. Masters simply increased the pressure. The horse capitulated and backed up, and Masters led his riders from the yard at a hard gallop.

Sharon slowly lowered her rifle. The door slammed and Tim came racing out with his shotgun. When he reached Sharon, he let her pull him close to her and hug him as they grimly watched Masters and his riders vanish into the timber.

"What'll he do if you don't clear out?" Longarm asked.

"He'll burn us out. Justin is in Crystal City. It is too late for me to get him, and it wouldn't do any good if I did. He is only one man."

"But isn't this your land?"

"No. Legally, it belongs to Masters. Months ago we sent our claim to Ottawa. But it hasn't come back. It never will. This is Masters's land now—or so he says."

"You better explain this to me."

"There is little to explain. Our people purchased our lands from the Indians generations ago. But now that we are part of Canada, Ottawa has sent out men to survey the land again. They disregard our boundaries and divide our lands into rectangular lots. In this way they contest our claims and take our land. We complain, but it does no good. Because Indian blood flows in our veins, we are dirty."

"In your veins also, Sharon?"

"Yes. And Tim's as well. My mother's grandmother. Her blood is the best part of us," she said proudly.

"And this warning from Masters . . . you take it seriously. He will burn you out?"

"For a year now, this is what happens if the Metis do not give up their land willingly."

"What about the Mounted Police?"

"The Metis would not go to them. They are English, like those who oppress us. Besides, what good would it do? We never have enough witnesses after the English strike."

"I think maybe tonight will be different. Maybe after tonight, we'll have something to show the Mounted Police."

Tim brightened. "You mean we're going to fight back?"

Longarm shook his head. "No, Tim. I'm afraid we could not stop that many riders. But perhaps we might be able to deliver a few of them to the Mounted Police. It might stir things up a bit."

"Then you will help us?" Sharon said eagerly.

"Of course."

"But you are not one of us."

"Let's stop all this jabbering and get ready."

She smiled, her white teeth brilliant in her dusky face, her dark eyes suddenly filled with gratitude. Longarm was pleased, too. He had a chance now to pay these two back for saving his life. If he could capture Masters in the act, the authorities would have no choice but to charge him, and even if Masters managed to elude prosecution, it would sure as hell put a crimp in his activities.

Somewhere in all this Longarm was hoping to find a bank robber—a man he had last seen poling frantically for the far shore, leaving his own men to fend for himself, a man who just might be Rene Dupre.

But that would have to come later.

Half an hour or so before midnight, the three took their positions. Tim, armed with his shotgun, was stationed in the fork of a tree that towered over the front yard. Longarm was at the edge of the clearing behind an oak, all six chambers of his .44 loaded, a Winchester rifle in his hand. Sharon, armed with a carbine, waited in thick bushes a hundred yards or so from the house.

Three saddled horses were waiting for them in a gully a good distance from the house. The flatbed wagon was there also, two dray horses already hitched in the traces. It was packed solidly with Sharon's most precious possessions, along with stores of food and clothing. The rest of the horses and the milch cow had been driven off into the surrounding timber to fend for themselves. Sharon had cried when she saw the cow disappear into the brush, its bell tinkling forlornly. The last of the livestock to go was her small flock of Rhode Island Reds. Longarm helped Tim chase them, squawking and fluttering indignantly, into the woods.

John Masters was punctual. At midnight his riders thundered through the timber, then broke into the clearing. Every rider's gun was out, and their faces were glowing in the light from their torches. With Masters in the lead, they pulled up in the clearing before the small ranch house. On Longarm's suggestion, Sharon had lit a single lamp and set it in a window so the riders would think they were inside.

"All right, you breeds!" Masters cried. "Come out of there!"

There was no response. Masters unlimbered his sixgun and fired at the window with the lamp in it. The rest pulled up alongside him and began firing into the same window. At last the lantern went flying. There was a slight *whump* from within the house, and a moment later flames appeared in the shattered window.

"Come out or burn!" Masters thundered.

The door did not open.

"Kill them all, damn them!" Masters cried. "Send them to hell!"

As he spoke, he flung his torch. It landed on the roof. Instantly the wood shingles caught. More torches arched through the night. Some landed on the roof, others on the porch. A few went blasting through the windows. As soon as the house was completely ablaze, the riders swept toward the two barns, flinging their torches as they rode past. The hayloft in the largest barn caught, then the roof. A feed shed went up next. The sudden roar of the flames cut off the sound of the horses' hoofs as the men rode about the yard, flinging their torches.

A hot wind came up from the direction of the blazing buildings, scorching and terrible in its intensity. Their shoulders hunched protectively, the night riders pulled to a halt around Masters and watched the buildings burn. They seemed to be expecting Sharon and her brother to come rushing out at any minute, despite the impossibility of it.

With an eager roar, a single sheet of flame engulfed the small farmhouse. For a moment the framing stood out clearly, valiantly—then vanished. Borne on the searing updrafts, sparks and flaming embers were swept into the night sky. A few horses whinnied frantically as they felt the waves of shimmering heat beating at them. Their riders had difficulty holding them in check.

Longarm stepped out from behind the tree and covered Masters with his Winchester. "All right, Masters!" Longarm told him. "Hold it right there!"

"You fool, Barker!" Masters cried. "What are you up to?"

"That's what I should be asking you, Masters! And I think maybe it's what the Mounted Police will be asking when I bring you and your bully boys in. Even this far from Ottawa, there must be laws against this sort of thing."

"Now, see here," Masters cried above the roar of the flames. "Maybe we can discuss this like sensible men!"

"Sure," Longarm told him. "Once you and your night riders drop your weapons and dismount."

Masters pulled his horse back. His face was grim with resolve and scathing in its contempt. "Not on your life!"

he retorted. "We'll not put our weapons down for you or anyone else!"

A rider beside Masters, as foolish as he was arrogant, flung up his sixgun and fired at Longarm. The bullet bit into the tree beside Longarm. Instinctively, Longarm flung his Winchester around and pulled the trigger. The slug entered the rider's mouth, punching a dark flower of brain and bone out through the back of his skull. As the rider tumbled back off his horse, Masters and the remaining riders opened up on Longarm.

Longarm ducked back behind the tree. Four slugs whacked into it. He cursed. This was not what he had planned. Tim's shotgun boomed twice, and then came the sharp crack of Sharon's carbine. Horses whinnied shrilly. A rider swore. Longarm peered out from behind the tree. In the hellish glow from the burning buildings, he saw clearly a rider peeling off his horse. Another thrown rider was crawling for cover on his hands and knees. The rest of the riders were in a panic. A mob on horseback, they milled about wildly, flinging shots into the darkness, some even into the flaming barns.

Masters had caught sight of Tim. As he aimed up into the tree, Longarm flung up his rifle and fired. Dropping his revolver, Masters slumped forward over his pommel. Spooked, his horse leaped ahead, then galloped back into the timber. The remaining riders, at least two of them severely wounded, took after Masters. A few minutes later, abandoning their three fallen comrades, Masters and his militia disappeared.

Longarm stepped out into the front yard. The barns were completely ablaze now, the leaping flames sending a lurid glow over everything, especially the three men on the ground. Skirting the rider he had killed, Longarm approached the second wounded man. Lying on his back with

38

his eyes closed, the fellow was clutching at a hole in his chest. He was breathing rapidly. A thin line of blood was trickling from one corner of his mouth. He would not last much longer.

Sharon and a somber Tim joined him as he went down on one knee beside the third downed rider. This one was lying face down. When Longarm turned him over, Sharon gasped. The dead man's lower jaw and most of his throat was gone. His eyes, wide in terror, were fixed on death.

Tim, his face pale, grimaced and looked quickly away.

"So much for my plan to take Masters to the Mounted Police as my prisoner."

"They just started shootin'!" Tim exclaimed. "They didn't give you a chance!"

"Shall we bury these men?" Sharon asked.

"We have no time," Longarm told her. "Masters will send one of his lieutenants back for them, anyway. You and Tim have got to get out of here. There'll be warrants issued. You and Tim'll be fugitives until we can get this cleared up."

"And you too, Ned," Sharon reminded him. "You are part of our struggle now."

Longarm nodded ruefully and looked at the three dead men. Their sprawled bodies seemed to tremble in the light of the burning buildings. These three night riders were sure enough dead. It did not really matter much that they had been the first to open fire. There would be little chance to make such fine distinctions if any one of them got caught by the Mounted Police. Masters and his men had simply been moving in to take possession of what legally belonged to them.

It was slightly unnerving. Longarm had been on the right side of the law for so long that it was not easy for him to realize that this night, in a few short minutes, he had crossed over to the other side—and in a country where his badge gave him little or no advantage. He was one hell of a long way out of his jurisdiction.

"Let's go," he told Sharon and Tim. "We've got horses and a wagon waiting and a long ride ahead of us."

Chapter 4

Sharon had described Crystal City as a Metis stronghold. Longarm could see why when they rode in three days later. Almost every sign was in French.

As they rode down the narrow main street, all normal activity ceased. The men and women on the sidewalks halted in their tracks. Others came out of stores to watch them ride by. Longarm dismounted in front of the livery stable and led his and Sharon's horses into the stable. Tim pulled the wagon to a halt at a hitch rack alongside the livery. By the time Longarm rejoined Sharon and Tim on the sidewalk in front of the livery stable, a crowd of grim-looking spectators had gathered.

Strangers were sure as hell not very welcome in Crystal City.

Sharon looked nervously at Longarm. Longarm shrugged. These were her people. What was she worried about?

"You are so tall," she whispered.

Then he realized what the problem was. It was Longarm who had drawn the crowd. He was obviously not a Metis. He looked like so many of their contemptuous oppressors —a tall Englishman. The enemy.

"Before they hang me from the nearest tree," Longarm told her, "tell them I'm not English. I'm an American."

The necessity for that vanished, however, when a bearded fellow broke through the sullen ring of men and hurried toward Sharon, a broad, pleased smile on his swarthy face.

"'Sharon!" he cried.

"Justin!"

Tim and Sharon ran to Justin. After their excited greeting, Sharon quickly explained things to her brother. Longarm saw Tim eagerly adding details. When the two had finished, Justin approached Longarm, smiling broadly. He shook Longarm's hand, then turned to the crowd. In a mangled French Longarm could barely follow, he attested enthusiastically to Longarm's pedigree. Obviously relieved, the crowd dispersed.

Justin had a place outside of town and insisted that Sharon and Tim go there with him. When Longarm asked about the local hotel, Justin assured him it was clean and then escorted him to it. In his swim across the river, Longarm had lost his wallet. Magnanimously, Justin advanced Longarm more than enough money to cover his hotel expenses. Longarm thanked him, then said goodbye to Sharon and Tim. An ancient bellhop who looked as if he would collapse before he reached the second floor showed Longarm to his room.

Longarm slumped on the bed, stared up at the ceiling, and took stock. Or tried to.

A telegram to Marshal Vail from this place would be a

dead giveaway, just as it would have been in Moosehead. Longarm could not approach the Canadian authorities from this Metis stronghold. He would just have to bide his time and pretend to go along with their politics.

From now on it was as Ned Barker that he would have to live or die, and that meant changing some. More than a few renegades had found the Canadian prairies a fine place to hide from the long reach of the U. S. marshals, and among most fugitives by this time, Longarm's tactics as well as his rawboned appearance were pretty well known.

He decided that he would no longer carry his derringer attached to his fob chain. It might better rest inside the back of his right boot. He would do well to retire his hidden cross-draw rig and rely instead on a simple open-top holster carried on a gunbelt. No longer would he wear a vest, and he would get himself a sheepskin coat to replace his frock coat. This last was not a difficult decision. It was already well into November and getting pretty damn chilly in this part of the world, especially after sundown. The mountain ranges to the northwest were already gleaming white at sunset.

Then, because at the river he had not only lost his wallet, but all the money he had taken with him, he would have to get himself a job. Finally—and this would not be easy for him—he would shave off his mustache.

Longarm shook his head unhappily at the thought, wondering which would be the most difficult thing for him to do—getting a job or shaving off his mustache.

A couple of days later, clean-shaven and snug in a sheepskin jacket, Longarm paused on the hotel porch to watch as the stage rocked into town. Something was wrong, he noticed at once. The driver was slumped over the brake lever and the coach was empty of passengers.

Then Longarm saw the bullet holes in the panels. He descended the porch steps. A crowd had already gathered in front of the express office. As the driver managed to pull his team to a halt, men swarmed up onto the bench to help the wounded man down.

As they carried him into the express office, he gasped out his story. Four masked men had held up the stage a few miles out of town. When the driver tried to stop them, he had been shot for his trouble. The holdup men had taken the money box, then robbed the six passengers and left them afoot.

At once the sheriff formed a posse and galloped out of town in an attempt to track the highwaymen. Longarm watched them ride out, then went back to the hotel porch. He found a chair and lit a cheroot. Then he waited.

The town was still in a turmoil when the six passengers —five men and the wife of one of the men— limped into view about an hour later. As they trudged wearily up the porch steps and into the hotel, Longarm looked them over carefully. Not one of the men, as far as Longarm could judge, was a Meti.

By this time the stage driver was resting comfortably in a room above the barber shop. The town doctor had already probed for and removed the slug in the stage driver's shoulder. According to what Longarm overheard from his vantage point on the hotel porch, this doctor liked to work with an evil-smelling solution of carbolic acid and water and was forever washing his hands and instruments in it. Furthermore, unlike most surgeons, who preferred to give their patients whiskey and operate as swiftly as possible, the doctor used chloroform and took his time when he operated. Few if any of his patients ever got an infection after one of the Doc's operations. Still, the townspeople shook their heads at his unorthodox methods.

After escorting the six passengers into the hotel, the manager of the stage's express office was leaving the hotel when Longarm got up from his chair and intercepted the small, bespectacled man.

"I'd like a job," Longarm told him.

"A job?"

"Shotgun rider. Looks like you need one around here."

"Not until now."

Longarm smiled. "Don't you figure maybe the time's come? How much money was in that strongbox?"

The manager was about to tell Longarm, but he caught himself. "That's company business," he said. "I'm not at liberty to divulge the amount."

"Suit yourself. But maybe it would be a good idea to wire the main office and see if they want a shotgun messenger." Longarm smiled. "If you get a favorable response, I'm available."

The manager raised his eyebrows as he considered Longarm's proposal. Then he nodded his head vigorously. "By grannies, I'll do that," he said. "Where will you be?"

Longarm smiled. "Right here."

He went back to his seat on the porch, lit another cheroot, and watched the manager head for the telegraph office.

That evening, while Longarm was sipping a beer in the saloon across from the hotel, Justin entered and walked over to his table.

"Sit down," Longarm told him amiably enough.

Justin pulled out a chair and slumped into it, his dark eyes regarding Longarm warily. "I just heard," he said. Like Sharon and his brother Tim, he spoke with a heavy accent.

"Heard what?"

45

"You been hired by the stage line to ride shotgun."

"Guilty as charged," Longarm said.

"Why do you do this?"

"Hell, I got to live, Justin. I can't keep on borrowing from you. You've been more than generous. Besides, looks to me like this stage line could use a man riding shotgun."

"Maybe you will not need to ride shotgun."

Longarm shook his head. "I just told you, Justin. I need the money."

"Join us instead."

"You?"

"We have trouble north of here. Near Rock Lake. I ride out tomorrow to join the rest of our people. Ride with me. Join us. Already you have struck a blow for our people. We can use a man like you." He smiled. "Besides, it is best for you to stay with us."

"Oh? Why is that?"

"You are a wanted man. Masters and his gunmen will be after you now. Before long, the Mounted Police will be looking for you, too."

Longarm shrugged. "Hell, look at it this way: The Mounties won't be looking for a man riding shotgun on the local stage."

"When do you start this job?"

"First thing tomorrow morning."

Justin leaned close. "How much will they pay you?"

Longarm told him.

Justin laughed. "My people will pay you twice that."

"You Metis got that much?"

"For a good man, we got it. By God, you bet."

Longarm looked carefully at Justin. "All this money—where do you get it from? You got a gold mine somewhere?"

Justin grinned. "The English. They are our gold mine."

"Like those English on today's stage?"

Justin leaned back in his chair and shrugged. "Now, how would I know such things?" Then he smiled.

It was just as Longarm had suspected. A Meti gang had held up the stage. Longarm had protested enough, he figured. He would most likely find Rene Dupre at Rock Lake. He shrugged. "All right, Justin. You talked me into it. Looks like I'll have to go over there to the express office and resign my new job. Too bad."

"I will go with you," Justin told him, getting to his feet.

Longarm had never really had a chance to refuse, he realized. Justin had come over to his table not to ask Longarm to enlist, but to draft him for the Meti cause, whether Longarm wanted to join up or not.

There was a soft rap on his door. Longarm flung aside the sheets, reached under his pillow for his .44, and called out softly, "Who is it?"

"Me."

It was Sharon's voice.

Surprised, Longarm padded on bare feet to the door and pulled it open. Sharon ducked quickly into the room. Longarm closed the door behind her.

"You don't need that, Ned," she told him when she saw the revolver in his hand.

As he lowered it, she stepped closer and put her arms around him. He bent his head and kissed her on the lips. She tightened her arms about him and leaned her body hungrily into his.

When they parted, she whispered huskily, "My God, Ned. Ever since I gave you that bath, I've been thinking of you. Wanting you."

"What the hell do you think that did to me?"

She laughed, delighted. "I thought so."

47

He pulled her over to the bed and put the revolver down on the nightstand. By that time, she had managed to step out of her dress and then her shift. She had come prepared, it seemed. There was no corset under the shift to slow either of them down.

"Now it's time for me to thank you properly for all you did,' she told him fiercely. "I shall never forget the way we drove off Masters and his night riders!"

Then she kissed him again, hungrily, her lips opening to his, working frantically. He ran his hand down her back, then under her to the warm moisture between her trembling thighs. She groaned softly as Longarm parted her knees with his own. Rolling gently onto her, he moved up slightly and slipped into her.

She gasped and moved her face to one side. Clinging fiercely to him, she locked her thighs about his waist and lunged upward, shuddering. In a moment they were both lunging eagerly, surging toward release. When it came, she gasped. He let go also, but stayed inside her, feeling himself grow large again almost immediately. He pulled her roughly toward him until he was probing deep into her once again.

She laughed, delighted. This time more gently, without the savage urgency of a moment before, they began to move again rhythmically as their heaving flesh got better acquainted. Before long she was moaning softly, her fingernails raking down his back. She shuddered convulsively under him, then tightened her arms about his neck. At last, uttering a high, sharp cry, she climaxed.

Longarm kept on thrusting. Clinging weakly to him, Sharon's cry died, and then she began to laugh and thrust upward again, groaning with pleasure, her mouth open, her eyes closed. She raked his back, thrust upward, and climaxed, clinging to him, shuddering wildly. To prevent herself from crying out this time, she bit into the flesh of his chest and clung to him. He felt a warm trickle of blood moving down over one nipple—and then felt himself coming also, in a powerful explosion.

They were lying side by side, a light patina of perspiration covering them both. As Sharon clung to Longarm, he had the queer notion that the two of them had just finished climbing a mountain together. It felt that good.

"Just tell me one thing," Longarm said.

"What's that?"

"Why did you wait so long? Do you know what condition I was in after that bath?"

"Do you know what condition *I* was in? But Tim was due back any minute. I could not risk having him burst in on us with a basketload of green apples."

"I suppose. But later—that night."

"That house was so small. And Tim is a very light sleeper."

"You are forgiven."

She kissed him on the lips, then caught his lower lip with hers, her tongue running swiftly across the inside of it, sending a shock of desire racing through his body clear down to his loins. Amazed, he felt himself jump to attention.

She laughed seductively and rolled over on top of him.

"I have a long ride ahead of me tomorrow," he warned her.

"Poor dear," she said, sinking onto his straining erection, her warm, luxuriant moistness enveloping it completely. "But do not worry. This will make you sleep well, and make you much lighter, too."

"You are so good to me," he gasped.

"It is not you I am thinking of," she told him. "It is your horse."

Longarm closed his eyes. This was no time for conversation.

As Sharon was leaving, Longarm asked her to do him a favor.

"Name it," she said without hesitation.

He walked over to the bureau and took from its top drawer his watch and the gold chain depending from it. The derringer he had already unclipped from the chain. Placing the watch and chain inside the pocket of his cross-draw holster, he wrapped them in his vest and frock coat and handed them to her.

"Keep these for me, will you?"

She took the bundle. "You will not need the watch?"

"It doesn't keep good time now. I guess it was that swim I took."

"That's too bad."

There was an awkward silence, as if she had something to say, but was reluctant to mention it. She glanced down at the floor.

"How will you get home?" he asked, mostly to break the awkward silence.

"My horse is tied up behind the hotel."

"Thank you for coming, Sharon."

"I might not see you again," she said unhappily.

He nodded and opened the door for her. She was almost through it when she paused and pulled back. Then, as if finally coming to a tough decision, she closed the door firmly and faced him. "Ned, you must be very careful," she said.

"Why do you say that?"

"Justin says you are not what you seem. You are an American—a very strong, unusual American. You are not like the others, those ill-bred outlaws who come here flee-ing warrants or the hangman's rope."

"And what do you say?"

"It is true. You are not like those others. They are filthy and they talk and drink like animals. They sleep with any-one who will let them near. You are not like them. Yet you do not use your own name."

Longarm was astonished. "Why do you say that, Sharon?"

She shrugged. "It does not seem to me that Ned Barker is your name."

"Why not?"

"It is in the way you act when I call you. There is always a slight hesitation. You have to remind yourself that Ned is your name. And when you were sick with the fever and I called your name, you did not respond. It had no meaning for you."

Longarm decided not to deny it. There was no reason to. After all, for a man not to go by his own name was not all that unusual in these parts.

He smiled at her and shrugged. "You've found me out," he admitted. "But for now I'll go by Ned Barker, if it's all right with you."

"It does not matter to me, Ned. But there is something you should know. My brother and many of our leaders have friends in Ottawa and also in the United States. We have learned much this way. What we know for sure is that a U. S. marshal is coming here from Denver to arrest one of our leaders."

"One of your leaders?"

"Yes. Rene Dupre."

"I know nothing of this, Sharon."

"Perhaps not. But Justin is not so sure. He thinks maybe you are this U. S. marshal. I tried not to think of this until now when I see how you have changed yourself. You gave me your watch just now, but kept the little gun. You shaved off your mustache and you wear your gun in a different way. Now you don't wear your coat and vest. You wear a sheepskin coat instead."

"This is a cold country, Sharon—and getting colder."

"Yes, that is true. It is what I told Justin." She went up on her tiptoes and kissed him on the lips, hard, with an urgency that surprised him. "Be careful, my long-legged one. There are wolves all around you."

Then she was gone.

Chapter 5

They were within a few miles of Rock Lake when the silence was broken by a rifle's sudden crack. Justin slipped from his horse, a startled look on his face, a bullet in his back.

Leaping from his own horse, Longarm snaked his Winchester from the saddle boot. With his other hand he dragged Justin into the cover of boulders along the trail. As Longarm pulled him roughly over the stony ground, Justin was squinting past Longarm's shoulder.

"I see them," he croaked feebly. "I see the bastards."

Longarm glanced back. The ridge above them was alive with riders. There were at least ten of them piling down the steep slope, intent on getting close enough to finish them off.

"Who the hell are they?" Longarm asked.

"Recruits, from the look of them."

"Recruits? You mean army men?"

53

"No. They've been hired by the English who want our land. Most of them come from the States. Gunslingers, you Americans call them." He grimaced suddenly from pain and leaned his head back against a boulder, his eyes shut tightly.

Longarm pulled Justin forward to examine his wound. He did not like what he saw. The hole was big and ugly, with dark blood pulsing slowly from it. It was close to the spine. "How do you feel?" he asked.

"Not so good. Already I am losing feeling in my legs. It is a bad wound. I am finished. Save yourself before they reach us."

"You ain't dead yet, and I'm not abandoning you."

Justin grabbed his forearm. "I tell you, go! Save yourself!"

"And I'm telling *you* I'm not leaving without you."

Justin closed his eyes and leaned his head back. "I have misjudged you, Ned," he gasped. "Forgive me."

"What the hell are you talkin' about?"

"I thought you were someone working against us."

"That's crazy talk."

"I know that now."

"Just stop talking. Save your breath. You're going to need it."

Justin nodded.

There was a low saddleback just ahead of the rocks. Over this a rider charged. His recklessness was an affront to Longarm. His Winchester barked. The rider toppled from his horse. Behind him came two more riders, bent low over their horses' necks, their sixguns blazing. But the fools were holding their barking sixguns too close to their mounts' heads. The alarmed horses bucked and veered wildly. One man was flung out of his saddle. The other gunslick, his horse rearing and kicking at the moon, fought to stay in the saddle. Longarm tracked him coolly and picked him off. Two more riders raced over the saddleback, saw what their three comrades had encountered, and promptly galloped back the way they had come.

Longarm looked down at Justin. He was unconscious. Longarm shook him. Justin's eyes flickered open.

"I've driven them off," he told Justin. "If we can get you back onto your horse, we can reach those friends of yours in Rock Lake after all."

Justin knew better. He shook his head feebly.

Ignoring the man's protests, Longarm flung him over his shoulder and raced out of the shelter of the rocks to their horses. He tied Justin face down over his saddle, then mounted up, leading Justin's horse after him into the timber. Behind him he heard hoofs thundering over the hogback. He swore. The bastards had not yet had enough.

He would have to fort up first chance he got.

He found a spot overlooking the trail with a clear line of fire for hundreds of yards down the slope in either direction. He had carried Justin into a small cave in the rocks behind him. He had tethered their horses in a small patch of brush and grass behind the cave. Crouched behind two large boulders, Justin's weapons on the ground beside him, Longarm waited for his pursuers to come into view.

He did not have long to wait.

Despite the toll Longarm had taken earlier, there were still eight riders. Their eagerness to kill Justin and Longarm impressed the tall deputy. What was so important about Sharon's quiet brother? he wondered.

Tracking the rear rider, Longarm squeezed the trigger. As the gunslick yanked back on his horse and tumbled crookedly from his saddle, Longarm swung his rifle ahead to the lead rider, who was already leaping from his horse. Longarm tracked him quickly and squeezed off a shot. The round caught him high and spun him violently to the ground. By then the others had leaped from their mounts and were digging for cover on the steep slope.

"Hey, you up there!" one of the riders called. "We don't want you! It's that damned Meti we want!"

"Why?"

"That's our business."

"You'll take him over my dead body!"

"Have it your way!"

A steady fire opened up on Longarm from the slope below. The rounds whined shrilly off the two boulders behind which he was crouching. He kept his head down and watched for gunflashes to help him locate the men closest to him on the slope below. He located two men pretty high up on the slope, the tops of their heads barely visible as they crouched behind a low embankment.

The firing let up. Longarm heard voices as the men shouted to each other. They were getting ready to charge up the slope. Longarm levered a fresh cartridge into the chamber of Justin's Winchester and checked the load of Justin's revolver. Then he braced himself, his rifle pointing down the slope at the nearest of the two gunslicks.

A muffled shout broke the sudden stillness. Longarm heard men's boots scrambling on gravel. Then the closest gunman, the one Longarm had already spotted, rose from behind the embankment. Aiming quickly, Longarm fired. The fellow went pinwheeling back down the slope. Longarm moved the rifle a fraction to the right just in time to catch the other one. He was laboring mightily as he struggled up the slope, head down, sixgun out. Longarm caught the fellow in his chest. He stopped, a look of amazement on his face, then collapsed face down, vanishing from sight.

Longarm heard shouts of dismay. Immediately the

charge evaporated. A few backs were visible as the men plunged back down the slope into the timber beyond. Longarm sent a few shots after them with no hope of doing damage. He just wanted them to hear the slugs rip into the branches over their heads.

The slope went silent again.

Longarm glanced up at the sun. It would not be long before the slope and the timber beyond were lost in twilight. When darkness came, Longarm decided, he might be able to slip away with Justin. That was his hope, anyway.

He began checking his loads in preparation for the next rush.

It did not come from the slope below him, but from his flanks. Longarm was less successful and the singing lead forced him back to the cave. As the bullets ricocheted about inside the cave, he kept his head down and waited. At last the firing subsided. There was a wait, then Longarm heard the same voice he had heard before, this time coming from the rocks above the cave.

"You in there, mister?"

Longarm said nothing.

"Come on out if you are, and we'll let you go. All we want is that damned Meti."

Longarm smiled and crouched lower, holding both six-guns. Next came a hurried consultation. Longarm could imagine the conversation. Some were for leaving him be, others for making a rush at the cave entrance. The talking ended and for a few minutes there was only silence. Then a rock rolled off the ledge above the cave, bounced in front of the entrance, and vanished down the slope.

A second later two men dropped into view. Crouching, they fired into the cave. Longarm returned the fire and rolled into a corner. For a few seconds the cave was filled with the detonations of all three men firing rapidly. The two gunmen, hit, toppled out of sight. Longarm's ears were ringing fiercely.

"Damn you, mister!" their leader called. "You ain't goin' free now! We'll stay here till hell freezes over. We'll starve you out!"

Longarm did not waste any breath responding. It was an empty boast, he knew. These men did not have the character or the patience for a long waiting game. They saw the world in small blocks of time. And they had wounded comrades to see to. Already Longarm could imagine the heated arguments for pulling out.

Longarm crept to the cave entrance and peered out. A rifle cracked from the rocks above him. He ducked. A shard of rock sliced past his skull as the round slammed into the rock face beside him. He moved back into the cave. It would be dark soon. He could wait until then before making his move.

He nudged Justin. There was no response. He rested the back of his hand against Justin's neck, near the jugular. The artery lay silent in cold flesh. Then Longarm saw the dark puddle under the dead man's skull. Exploring it with his hand, he felt the hole where the ricocheting bullet had entered.

Longarm had been defending a dead man. He swore softly, then pulled Justin's body to the cave entrance and waited for darkness to fall. When it did, and before the moon rode into the sky, Longarm propped Justin up against the damp wall just inside the cave entrance. He placed the man's rifle in his arms and pulled his hat down over his dead eyes.

Then he slipped out of the cave and started through the rocks to where he had left their horses. He was careful, circling the small grassy area twice before approaching his horse and swinging up into the saddle. He was riding slowly back down through the timber when a horseman appeared on his right and one on his left. Before he could draw his sixgun, a rider came up from his right and swung the barrel of his Colt. The blow caught Longarm on the side of his head and he went tumbling backward off the horse.

He hit the ground and remembered nothing.

He awoke blinking at the bright morning sunlight. He was propped up against a tree and a campfire was blazing close by him. His wrists were bound in rawhide so tight his hands were throbbing dully. They sat in his lap like dirty, swollen turnips. Even if he could perform the necessary contortions that would enable him to pull the derringer from his boot, his swollen fingers would be unable to cock and hold the weapon.

"Well, well," said a voice beside him. It belonged to the gunslick who had demanded his surrender earlier.

Longarm turned. A fellow with a cruel, pocked face was hunkered down beside him. His eyes were cold, his mouth a flat, contemptuous line, his face covered by a dark stubble. About his neck he had tied a filthy polka-dot bandanna. He was wearing greasy Levi's and a checked shirt. From his vest pocket dangled a Bull Durham tag. A carelessly built cigarette hung from his lips. Chucking the brim of his hat back off his forehead, he squinted through the smoke at Longarm.

"So you ain't dead, after all," he drawled.

Two other men stepped up alongside the fellow with the pocked face. "What do you think, Rance?" one of them said. "Maybe we should finish him here?"

Rance grinned up at the man, his yellow teeth like fangs. "Maybe so, Lem. Maybe so."

"I say we make him walk," said the other one, his voice sharp with anger. Longarm could understand why. He was one of the men Longarm had wounded in the firefight. His left arm was resting in a makeshift sling.

"Keep cool, Karl," Rance told him, grinning. "You wouldn't've got hit if you'd kept your ass down."

Karl took a step back, his unhappy, glaring eyes still on Longarm.

Rance looked back at Longarm. "You got a pretty hard head, mister. Must be solid clean through."

Longarm considered Rance carefully. He was not Canadian. Maybe a Southerner, judging from his drawl—a Texas Southerner. "Untie me. Justin is the man you wanted, and now he's dead."

"Yeah, the Meti is dead. But you sure as hell didn't make it any easier for us. Who are you, anyway?"

"Name's Ned Barker."

"I think you're a liar."

"You can think anything you want."

"I think maybe you're a long-legged son of a bitch I heard about back in Texas—a U. S. marshal name of Custis Long."

"Never heard of him."

"Well, I heard plenty. He's supposed to be messin' around up here. And I know what he looks like. He has a longhorn mustache he's right proud of. And he's tricky enough. He wears a cross-draw rig under the skirt of his frock coat and carries a derringer in his vest pocket."

"Less'n you want to search me for a derringer, I guess that lets me out."

"Maybe it does, maybe it don't. You could've changed your clothes. And from the color of your upper lip, I can tell you just shaved off a mustache. Besides that, there

60

ain't no doubt you're from the States. And you're sure as hell big and rangy enough."

"That don't make me a goddamn U. S. marshal."

Longarm glanced up at the angry circle of men peering down at him. Not a one was smiling, and more than a few in addition to Karl were bandaged pretty heavily. One man was leaning on a makeshift cane. He had sure as hell mauled this outfit, Longarm told himself, feeling some satisfaction. But why they hadn't already killed him in retaliation was a wonder.

"Then what're you doin' up here?" Rance demanded.

"You mean in Canada?"

"You know what I mean."

"I'm hired out to the Metis. They're expecting trouble. And it looks like you're the trouble. If Masters can hire gunmen, why can't the Metis?"

"Well, this looks like the end of your employment, then. You're done workin' for the Metis."

"So maybe I could work for Masters."

"Why don't you ask him? Fact is, that's why I kept you alive."

"I was wondering why you didn't kill me."

"I still think we should," Karl barked angrily.

Rance smiled coldly at Longarm. "You hear that, mister? We left two riders back there for the buzzards. But I ain't worried. You'll pay. Masters will see to that."

The gang leader stood up and tossed his cigarette away. Then he walked off toward the horses. Longarm looked past him and saw Justin's lifeless body tied over his horse, his wrists attached to his ankles by a rope passed under the horse's belly.

Someone kicked Longarm brutally. He looked up. It was Karl.

"Just wanted to get your attention," Karl said. "Get up and climb onto your horse."

Longarm struggled to his feet and boosted himself up into his saddle. Karl took the reins of his horse and mounted up himself. Grabbing the saddlehorn, Longarm hung on. The circulation in his hands was already so poor he was afraid they might get gangrenous before he reached wherever it was they were taking him.

But maybe he should worry about his neck, not his hands.

Someone kicked dirt on the campfire and they rode out, heading northwest into the timber.

As they rode, Longarm felt a deep and sullen exasperation. So much for secret government business. Everyone in Canada, it seemed, was aware that a U. S. marshal, Custis Long by name, was in the country. Longarm could understand the Metis being warned, since he was after Dupre. But why would Masters be concerned? Hell, Longarm was doing just what he wanted. His mission, after all, was to rid the province of a well-known Meti troublemaker.

Longarm remembered Sharon's words then. They seemed singularly appropriate. He *was* surrounded by wolves—and those wolves had already pulled down and devoured her brother.

Close to sundown, they approached a town the riders called Beaver Creek. Riding past a sawmill, they continued down a winding trail until they came to a swift mountain stream, then clopped across a plank bridge and rode onto Beaver Creek's main street. The small lumber town was crowded into a long, narrow valley, sheer mountain walls hemming it in on both sides. The wood shacks and buildings looked as if they had been slapped up hastily with little or no care for permanence. Everything was built of rough-cut timber;

the boardwalks, the hitch rails, the stores and feed mills. Strips of rotting bark were hanging from the edges of the saloon's sign. A damp, chill wind swept down from the peaks north of the town, and the smell of woodsmoke hung heavy in the air.

It was a closed-in, mean-looking place.

They kept on through the town. Rance's men, including those wounded who were able to get about without assistance, got leave from him to peel off at the single saloon. Rance, Karl, and Lem kept on, however, heading for a large, rambling log house on a rise beyond the town. Lem was leading the horse carrying Justin's body.

As they approached the house, a fellow carrying a rifle stepped out onto the porch. He was wearing dark trousers, a vest, and a white shirt. His thick, reddish hair was cut short, his sandy mustache drooping to his chin.

Pulling up before the porch, Rance said, "Howdy, Keller. We got that Meti. That's him, draped over his horse."

Keller's cold eyes lighted up slightly as he glanced over at Justin's limp body. "You done well, Rance," he said grudgingly.

Keller yelled for someone then, his voice sharp and commanding. An old man wearing a checked wool shirt and carrying a pitchfork came running from one of the barns. Keller told him to take care of Justin's body.

The man hesitated. "Take *care* of it, Mr. Keller?"

"Bury it, damn it! Bury the dead man on the horse Lem's leading."

The fellow with the pitchfork moistened his lips nervously. "Where do you want me to bury him?"

"Anywhere. In the manure pile, if you want. I don't care. Just bury the son of a bitch."

The fellow grabbed the reins of the horse carrying Justin's body and led him off. Keller glanced over at Longarm.

"Who's this one?" he asked Rance.

"He's a bonus. Justin's sidekick. His name's Ned Barker, the same one Masters has been screaming about— the one who messed him up at the river ranch."

"This him?" Keller asked, peering closer at Longarm. "Well, well. Bring the bastard in. Masters will sure be glad to see him."

"How is he?"

"He'll live. But his temper ain't improvin' none."

"You want me to stick around, see if he wants anything?"

"No," Keller said with brutal frankness. "If we need you, we'll know where to get you."

"Sure. Sure thing, Keller."

Rance pulled his horse around and told Karl to get Longarm off his horse. Then he and Lem rode back down the hill.

Dismounting, Karl yanked Longarm roughly to the ground. Longarm landed hard on his side, then got to his feet, his bound hands giving him no help at all. Karl grinned at Longarm's discomfort, grabbed his swollen wrists, swung him around, and booted him roughly up the steps and onto the porch.

Keller opened the door for Longarm and led him into the house, up a flight of stairs, and into a huge bedroom. Sitting in a chair by the window, a blanket thrown over his legs, sat John Masters. A thick white bandage was wrapped around his chest.

The sight of Longarm walking into the room startled Masters. Then his face brightened incredulously. "What is this, Keller? Christmas?"

"It's a bonus. Rance just rode in with him and the dead Meti, the one called Justin."

"As much as I hate the idea, I guess I'll have to congratulate that piece of shit."

"I already took care of it."

"Good. Then I won't have to go near him."

A young Indian housekeeper was piling supper dishes on a table behind Masters. When she glanced over at Longarm, he saw that she had large brown eyes, like dark flowers opening to the sunlight. She had a fresh, vital beauty that caught his attention at once. Returning his gaze, she dropped a heavy spoon. It clattered loudly, jarringly on the plank floor.

Masters turned in his chair to glare at her. "You damned fool!" he cried. "Haven't you got them dishes cleared away yet? God damn it! Looks like I'm right. You're good for only one thing! Now get the hell out of here!" Furious, he bent down and swept up a slipper and hurled it at her. She ducked, but it glanced off her shoulder as she hurried, terrified, from the room.

Still simmering, Masters looked at Keller. "You, too. Get out of here. Leave me alone with this meddling bastard. But stay close in case he tries anything."

Keller ducked out of the room.

"For just a minute I didn't recognize you, mister," Masters told Longarm. "You shaved off your mustache."

"Yes."

"And you look real comfortable in that sheepskin coat."

"Yes."

"Get over here," Masters said.

Longarm walked over to him. Slumped in his high-backed upholstered chair, he looked pale and gaunt. But the bullet Longarm had sent into him had done nothing to curb the man's arrogance.

"If this is your place, Masters," Longarm asked, "what did you need Sharon's ranch for?"

"That's my business, Mr. Custis Long."

Without changing his expression, Longarm cocked his head. "I already told you who I am: Ned Barker. Who is this Custis Long, anyway? And why am I supposed to be him?"

"After the doctor took your slug out of my shoulder, I got a message from the local Mounted Police. Seems they've been getting urgent signals from Ottawa. There's a Marshal Vail in Colorado who insists the Mounted Police find and cooperate with one of his federal marshals, Custis Long. This U. S. marshal has been sent up here to arrest Rene Dupre and take him back to the States. Something about robbing a bank in Wisconsin, I believe."

"That so?"

"Yes, Longarm. That's so."

"Longarm?"

"That's how he's known throughout the Rockies and points west. He's a man with a considerable reputation."

Longarm shrugged. "I wish I could oblige you, Masters, but I ain't him."

"I can understand your reluctance to admit who you are."

"You can?"

"Of course. It isn't legal, even for a U. S. mashal, to go around shooting up Canadian citizens. Such behavior could easily generate a serious rift between our two countries."

"You worried about rifts, are you?"

Masters shrugged.

"Fact is," Longarm drawled, "I'm clear on the other side of the law."

"On the run, are you?"

Longarm shifted his feet. "Ain't that what I said?"

"Yes, I can see where a man as ready to use a gun as you are might be in trouble with the law—assuming, of course, that you are not the famous Longarm I just mentioned."

"Well, I ain't. My name's Ned Barker, and I'm up here lookin' for work—any kind, so long as the pay is good."

"Any kind, you say?"

"You hard of hearing, Masters?"

"Tell me. Was it murder sent you into Canada, Barker? Or are you one of the James gang—a train robber?"

Longarm shrugged. "Whatever came to hand, Masters."

Masters nodded, intrigued. He seemed satisfied that Longarm was telling him the truth, that he was not the famous lawman, after all.

"Look, Masters," said Longarm, "I didn't mean to cut you or your men up, but you never left me no choice. Cut this rawhide off my wrists and I'll join up with your outfit."

"Yesterday you were riding with a Meti insurgent. Now you offer to ride for me. You change loyalties pretty fast. And this certainly was not the song you were singing when you stood beside that Meti woman. I wish she could hear you now. You're nothing but a turncoat, willing to sell your services to the highest bidder."

"So what if I am? I can ride as well for you as I can for the Metis."

Grimly, Masters shook his head. "No, you can't, Barker. You'll have to find some other way to save your neck—if you can. I swore I'd kill you, and I meant it. Look at me. You're the one who put me in this chair."

Longarm shrugged. "Sorry about that. It wasn't anything personal."

As he spoke, Longarm walked over to the table where the Indian had left the supper dishes. A long, serrated kitchen knife was resting on a plate. Longarm snatched it up and dropped it into the pocket of his sheepskin coat.

Masters twisted around painfully in his chair. "What are you doing over there?"

"There's food here. I'm hungry."

"Well, you won't be eating off my plates, Barker! Get back here!"

A .32 caliber revolver gleamed in Masters's hand. It must have been resting on his lap under the blanket. When Longarm did not move immediately, Masters cocked it. With an easy shrug, Longarm walked back to Masters.

"Nothing would please me better than to send a bullet into you right now, Barker," Masters said evenly.

"You know what, Masters? You talk too much."

The revolver in Masters's hand detonated. Longarm felt his hat fly back off his head, snapping its chin strap hard against his Adam's apple.

"One more time, you son of a bitch," Masters said. "Try my patience one more time."

"Hell, you're the one wanted to talk."

"Keller!" Masters called. "Get in here!"

The door opened and Keller burst through the doorway, his gun out.

"Get this bastard out of here. Put him in with the sled dogs, that bunch with Blackie."

"Blackie?"

"You heard me," he replied. "This way, you won't need to feed them for a while."

Hurrying up to Longarm, Keller pulled him roughly from the room. Downstairs, Keller pushed Longarm through the back door and then up onto a slight rise behind the house. Ahead of him, Longarm saw a series of long kennels encircled by a high chicken-wire fence. Keller unlocked the gate, dragged Longarm into the biggest kennel, then flung him inside and locked the door.

Longarm was too busy watching the sled dogs to see Keller leave. He had his eye on one in particular, a big black dog with a broad, powerful chest. This had to be the one they called Blackie. Half of his right ear had been torn off, and there was a mean-looking scar on the side of his snout. He rose slowly and menacingly to his feet and faced Longarm, his tail low, his lips curling back as he bared his teeth. A low growl came from deep in his chest.

There was no time to bend down and get the derringer out of his boot. Besides, the shot would alert the house. Longarm pulled the kitchen knife from his jacket pocket. At once the other sled dogs jumped to their feet and set up a furious, rapid barking. The unnerving chorus seemed to encourage Blackie. His fangs bared, he advanced on Longarm.

With both hands gripping the handle of the kitchen knife, Longarm backed slowly, waiting for the dog to charge.

Chapter 6

The dog leaped. Longarm felt the animal's forepaws strike his chest. The force of the charge sent Longarm reeling back. He tripped and fell, landing hard, the dog on his chest. Longarm could feel the animal's hot, searing breath as he lunged for Longarm's throat, his teeth clicking loudly as they snapped shut.

Twisting his head aside, Longarm brought the knife down. He felt the blade slice into the dog's back, but this only seemed to arouse the dog to a greater fury. Desperately, Longarm rolled over onto the dog, his bound hands forcing him to enclose the animal in a terrifying bear hug. His foul breath searing Longarm's face, the dog lunged repeatedly for Longarm's neck. Using the full weight of his body, Longarm crushed the dog down onto the floor as he continued to probe with his knife for a vulnerable spot.

He felt the blade slip past the dog's backbone and plunge deep. The dog yelped once, loudly, then thrashed feebly. A freshet of hot blood poured out over Longarm's bound wrists, the surge almost strong enough to rip the knife from his grasp. Whining softly, the dog went limp under him.

Longarm glanced at the other dogs. They were still barking furiously. In such a low-ceilinged, narrow structure, the sound of their infuriated, insane yelping was enough to make Longarm's scalp crawl. And they were closer now, their eyes wild with the scent of blood.

Longarm scrambled to his feet. Reaching down with his bound hands, he lifted Blackie's still warm carcass and flung him into the midst of the yapping dogs. The famished sled dogs pounced on their leader's remains, snarling viciously as they ripped the carcass to pieces and dragged portions of it away to their corners.

Burying the point of the knife into the wall, Longarm leaned his waist against the handle to brace it, then rubbed the rawhide still binding his wrists against the serrated edge. The rawhide separated. The blood surging into his hands caused a painful pins-and-needles reaction.

Watching the dogs warily, he rubbed his hands together to get the circulation back in them. The dogs sounded even more vicious devouring their leader than they had when barking at Longarm. He had heard that sled dogs out of their traces and left without work or exercise for any length of time became vicious, usually turning on the weakest member of their team or on any man careless enough to get too close. The only living creature that could handle the dog team at such times was its trace leader, since he was the only one crafty and vicious enough to mete out proper punishment.

Though now they were feasting on their leader's remains, it would not be long before they turned on each other—or on Longarm if he remained in their midst. Their blood lust was thoroughly aroused. Despite the excruciating pain in his wrists and hands, Longarm dropped the knife into the pocket of his sheepskin jacket, put his shoulder down, and slammed against the flimsy kennel door. It sagged open slightly, but held. He made another run at it. This time the door slammed open. He ducked out through it and quickly wound a strip of loose wire around the door post to keep it shut.

The sled dogs, still eagerly tearing at their deposed master, did not even look up.

It was a simple matter to force open the enclosure's gate. Night was falling swiftly now, a cold white moon riding high over the surrounding hills. Pulling the derringer from his boot, Longarm approached the house cautiously, then slipped in through the back door.

He found himself in a narrow hallway. Stairs in front of him led to the second floor. There were two doors to his right. He nudged one open slightly and saw the back of the Indian housekeeper as she cleaned up the kitchen. He pulled the door shut gently, then tried the next door. It led to a hallway leading past the staircase to the front door. Longarm moved swiftly down the hallway. He found a large living room to his right and ducked into it.

With a poker in one hand and a piece of firewood in the other, Keller was building a fire in the fireplace. The crackling of the flames covered the sound of Longarm's footsteps as he approached. Longarm had almost reached Keller before the man flung himself around. Without hesitation, he hurled the piece of firewood at Longarm. The chunk of wood sailed past Longarm's shoulder and crashed into the wall. Then, his poker held high over his head, Keller advanced on Longarm.

Longarm cocked the derringer.

"Fire that toy," Keller warned, "and the shot will bring the whole valley up here."

Longarm lowered his shoulder and flung himself at Keller. Keller swung the poker. It swished through the air inches over Longarm's head seconds before Longarm crunched into Keller's midsection. A sudden rush of air burst from Keller's lungs as the force of his charge sent the man hurtling backward. Keller's heel caught on the fireplace ledge and the back of his head crunched into the mantel. He jackknifed backward into the roaring flames. Before he could scream out in pain, Longarm clapped his big hand over Keller's mouth and continued to force him back into the fireplace. A moment later, his backside roasted, his pants and the back of his shirt on fire, he sagged loosely forward into Longarm's arms, unconscious.

Longarm dragged him out of the fireplace and stomped out the flames with his boots. Then he headed across the room to the wall rack where rifles and other firearms hung. The Indian housekeeper entered. She gazed calmly over at Keller's smoking figure, then at Longarm. For a long moment the two stood looking at each other. Then, without a word, the housekeeper went back to the kitchen.

Longarm took down his Winchester and checked the magazine. It was full. His Colt was lying on the top of the cherry bureau under the rack. He checked its load also and then the firing pin. He exchanged his kitchen knife for a huge bowie so sharp its blade seemed to melt the hairs off his arm as he passed it lightly over them. Next he pulled open the top drawers of the bureau and found what he had been hoping for—boxes of .44-40 shells. He grabbed as many as he could and jammed them into the big, wide pockets of his sheepskin jacket, then started for the stairs and John Masters.

Masters was not in his bedroom. Pausing in the hallway

outside it, Longarm thought he heard a woman crying. The soft, pitiful sound was coming from a room much farther down the hallway. Then he heard a woman's pleading voice. It was faint, but strangely, distantly familiar. Then came the ugly sound of a slap, bringing to a sudden halt the woman's entreaties.

Longarm hurried down the hall, came to the door, and kicked it open. As he strode in, he found Masters bent over a woman spread-eagled on the bed. She was naked, her wrists bound by bedsheets to the top posts, her ankles to the posts at the foot of the bed.

For an invalid, Masters looked healthy enough. He had flung his bathrobe to the floor and was straddling the woman, his scrawny buttocks bobbing comically as he tried to pin her struggling shoulders to the bed while attempting to penetrate her. All this Longarm saw in the instant the door swung open.

Masters froze, then flung a dismayed look over his shoulder. At the sight of Longarm, he flung himself off the woman, his eyes wide with fear and humiliation. To Longarm, it seemed it was mostly humiliation Masters was feeling at that moment. For a man of his pretensions, to be caught in this fashion was not at all pleasant. Indeed, it was degrading.

Striding into the room, Longarm glanced over at the woman. She struggled to lift her head, and when he saw her face, he almost pulled to a halt, he was so startled. The woman tied to Masters's bed was Andrea, the shrewd poker player he had met in Denver—the dark, exciting woman who had given him such a fond farewell.

She recognized Longarm as well. Tears of anger and frustration welled into her eyes. Ignoring Masters's crouching presence on the other side of the bed, Longarm flung the bedspread over Andrea's nakedness, then slashed through the bedsheets that bound her.

Andrea sprang off the bed, wrapping the bedclothes about her, her eyes flashing venom as she turned on Masters. "Kill him!" she breathed. "Kill him, Longarm! Kill the bastard!"

"I can't do that."

"Give me a gun. I'll do it."

"I don't think I can do that, either."

"Your knife, then!"

The housekeeper appeared in the doorway behind Longarm. He turned to her.

"Riders come," she said.

"Go downstairs. Don't let them in. Tell them I've escaped, that I've fled past the dog kennels, toward the mountains. Hurry."

She turned and vanished down the hallway.

Longarm looked back at Andrea. "Get dressed," he told her. "We're getting out of here."

Andrea hurried over to the closet and began pulling out her things. They had been thrown into a pile in a corner of the closet.

"You won't get far," Masters told them.

"Maybe not. But we're taking you with us for a hostage."

"I won't go."

Longarm walked up to him, measured carefully, then brought the barrel of his gun across the man's face. He went reeling into a corner. His hand held up to his swelling, bleeding cheekbone, he looked at Longarm in terror.

"You going to cooperate?" Longarm asked him.

"Let . . . let me get dressed."

Longarm spoke to Andrea. "Go with him to his room.

Make sure he dresses warmly. He won't be any good to us frozen to death."

Then he handed Andrea his derringer.

"You trust me with this?" she asked, taking it. "I might use it on him."

"I trust you. You know you can't expect any help from me if you kill him. And, like I said, he's more valuable to us alive than dead."

"All right," she said. "Just don't expect me to be easy on the son of a bitch."

Longarm chuckled. "All right. I won't."

Masters was still cowering in the corner. It was clear he did not put as much trust in Andrea's self-control as Longarm did. *Let him sweat*, Longarm decided. He left the bedroom and hurried back down the hall to the head of the stairs.

Below him the front door was open. The Indian girl was out on the porch, talking to Rance and two other riders.

Stealing softly down the stairs, Longarm flattened himself alongside the door and listened.

". . . just now he go," the housekeeper was telling them. "Mr. Masters and Mr. Keller, they go after him. Maybe you hurry so he not get away!"

"You sure of this, Blossom?"

"I hear the dogs bark when he go. I watch from window and see him. Then I tell boss man and Keller. You don't have to believe me. Go back to your whiskey if you want."

"Shut up, Indian," Rance snarled.

He turned to the others. "Let's go, boys. This time we'll bring that bastard back heel first!"

The three men turned their horses, then spurred past the barns and vanished around the corner of the house. Longarm moved swiftly through the kitchen and pushed open the back door. He was in time to see the three riders flash past the house, mount the rise, then—caught for a moment in the full flood of the moonlight—gallop out of sight beyond the dog kennels.

He turned. Blossom was standing beside him.

"I think I go with you," she said.

"Why?"

"I think maybe I lose my job here."

"Okay. Pack plenty of food. But we're going to have to do some hard riding to get out of this. Can you manage that?"

She brightened. "Blossom can ride. And she can cook. Anything else big man wants, she do that, too!"

Longarm laughed, then hurried past her and back upstairs.

Chapter 7

It was the next day, close to noon. Longarm was riding in the lead. Behind him came Andrea, leading Masters's horse. Masters's hands were tied behind his back, making it extremely difficult for him to stay in the saddle. That had been Andrea's idea. She had insisted it would take some of the starch out of him. It was doing just that.

Behind Masters rode Blossom, leading a pack horse loaded with provisions. She took great pleasure, it appeared, in watching Masters weave painfully on his saddle. Every once in a while Masters would plead for them to hold up so he could rest. He needed water, he told them. No one paid him the slightest attention.

They had ridden clear through the night on four of Masters's best horses. Even the pack horse Blossom was leading was a fine chestnut, good for a spare if they lost any of the four saddle horses. It had been chancy skirting around the lumber town the previous night without alerting anyone, but they had accomplished it by leading their horses and gagging Masters with a bandanna. Later, when they were well clear of the town, Masters had demanded to know where they were taking him. It was Andrea who had told him they were heading for Rock Lake.

"Riders behind us," Blossom called softly.

Longarm pulled his horse around and rode back to join her. Andrea halted also. Blossom pointed to the sky just above a hollow between the timbered foothills behind them. Longarm saw what appeared to be a faint cloud hanging low over the hills.

"That is dust of riders," she said.

"How many?"

"Six, maybe seven. No more."

As Longarm watched the patch of dust, it dissipated in the wind. In a moment the air above the timber was clear of any sign.

"Thanks, Blossom," he said.

Longarm rode back to the head of the column and kept going, his eyes searching the trail ahead intently. When he came to a patch of exposed cap rock, he held up to wait for Andrea and Blossom to come up to him.

"Blossom," he said, "you and Andrea follow this stretch of cap rock until you reach that timbered slope over there. Stay on the rock. I'll remain behind and do what I can to erase any sign."

She nodded and guided her horse and the pack horse gently up onto the rock, keeping to a walk so the horses' hoofs would not chip the surface. Andrea, leading Masters's horse, did the same. Longarm waited until they were out of sight in the timber, then dismounted.

Cutting off a pine branch, he moved back over their trail, brushing away any tracks. Then he mounted up, returned the way he had come, then rode boldly off in a more southerly direction. Eventually he came to a stream. He splashed into its cold waters and turned his horse upstream, heading in the direction Blossom had taken.

He found Andrea and Blossom waiting for him on a ledge overlooking the trail they had abandoned. One of them had wrapped a bandanna around Masters's mouth again to keep him from crying out.

"Who did that?" Longarm asked, dismounting.

"I did," Andrea said. "I wouldn't put it past the son of a bitch to cry out first chance he got."

"Good idea."

The three of them peered down through the timber, waiting for some sign of their pursuers. Before long they glimpsed through the trees a small group of riders pressing on, moving south along the false trail Longarm had provided. Blossom had been right on the money. There were seven riders in all. The bunch rode on without pause, vanishing into the timber.

"I think we can relax now," Longarm suggested. "For a while, anyway."

Blossom nodded. "I make meal."

"Don't show any smoke."

Blossom looked at him as if he had insulted her. "I not show smoke," she told him. "What you think?"

She was a Blackfoot, Longarm had learned during their brief stops to rest and water the horses. Though she could not have been more than twenty-five, she had already cooked for a couple of Meti trappers. A few English, too. The others she had liked, but Masters she despised. He was no better than skunk droppings, she told them, delighted that Masters, thoroughly gagged, was within earshot.

She prepared for them salt pork and beans, coffee so powerful it raised the hair on the back of Longarm's neck, and finished off the minor feast with sourdough biscuits that melted in their mouths, accomplishing all of it without a hint of smoke, just as she had promised.

Sipping his second honey-sweetened cup of coffee, Longarm called Andrea over and asked her to sit beside him. He had some questions he wanted answered. She did not protest. Wrapping a blanket around her to keep off the chill, she scrunched down beside him and leaned back against a tree.

"Kind of remarkable, wouldn't you say?" Longarm asked.

"You mean the way I turned up again like a bad penny."

"I didn't say you were a bad penny."

"It was inevitable once I learned you were the one they were sending after Rene."

"Rene Dupre?"

"Yes."

"Maybe so, but what in blazes were you doing tied to that bed?"

"A miscalculation."

"You want to explain that?"

"Sure. From Denver I went to Ottawa to see the lawyers representing our people."

"Lawyers?"

"They're trying to get our land claims accepted by the government, or at least give us enough time to present a petition to the courts. But they have not been very successful, so Rene sent me to find out what was causing the delay."

"You mean he had to send you there to find that out?"

"You're right. It should have been obvious all along. The lawyers have been delaying deliberately."

"More likely they were bought off," Longarm mused.

"That's close to it. They demanded more money."

"In American silver certificates?"

She cast an ironic glance at him. "Yes."

"Who is Rene Dupre to you, anyway?"

"He's my brother."

Longarm finished his coffee and flung the dregs into the bushes beside him.

"We got sidetracked, I guess," Longarm said. "You were telling me how it was you ended up on Masters's bed."

"In Ottawa, Masters was pointed out to me as one of the four or five men who have been selected to come out here and organize the English settlers against the Metis. I cultivated his acquaintance in order to find out what he was doing."

"The way you cultivated mine."

"Yes," she admitted frankly.

"But you weren't as successful."

"I was quite successful. Too much so. I got careless. During the stagecoach ride to here, he found me going through his papers. He beat me until I no longer saw any sense in not admitting what I had been doing."

"I see. How long were you in his place?"

"Long enough. A few weeks."

"I'm sorry, Andrea."

"I wish he had killed me. As it was, I was so weak I betrayed my own brother. I told Masters what I knew of Rene's plans to use the Bonaventure Mine."

"The Bonaventure Mine? I never heard of it," Longarm said.

"Few people have. We have been trying to keep it a secret. We knew once the word got out it would bring still more greedy English onto our land."

"Rich, is it?"

"It has immense resources of gold and silver. Rene knew that with that to finance us, we could hire as many mercenaries as we would need, and all the firepower as well. But Masters alerted the Mounted Police, and they drove our men away from the mine and claimed it for themselves."

"You wouldn't need to rob banks—and stagecoaches."

"That's right."

"Where are Rene and the rest of his men now?" Longarm asked.

"Rock Lake."

"That's why we're going there?"

"Yes."

"Not too long ago I was on my way to Rock Lake with Justin Robideau when Rance and his men overtook us."

"Justin?" Her eyes widened in surprise. "Is . . . is he all right?"

"Rance's men killed him."

Her face went white. She looked over at the sprawled, gagged figure of John Masters. For a moment he thought she was going to get up and strangle the man. Then she looked back at Longarm, the light gone from her eyes. "Long before all this trouble, Justin and I were engaged," she said simply.

Longarm kept silent, waiting for her to regain her composure. Then he asked, "You got any idea which bank in Wisconsin your brother might hit next?"

She looked bleakly at Longarm. "I know nothing about such things."

"But you knew enough to telegraph your fellow revolutionaries that I was heading for Moosehead—along with a pretty good description of what I looked like. They killed my Canadian contact and came within a whisker of killing me. Thanks a lot, Andrea."

She could not hide her discomfiture. "I am sorry, Longarm. Truly I am. But we are fighting for our existence as a people."

"Exception noted. If your friends kill me, it's nothing personal."

"You must believe that."

"Oh, I do. I assure you, it's a great comfort to me."

"Please, Longarm, there is really nothing I can do. But you must believe how grateful I am to you for getting me away from Masters."

"Sure thing, Andrea. And I'm sorry about Justin. I liked him."

She nodded wearily and got to her feet. Longarm watched her go, then got up also. It was time they pushed on. He was almost to his horse when Blossom intercepted him, her large eyes filled with concern.

"Soon we get big snow," she said.

Longarm glanced up at the sky. It was cloudless, as blue as a baby's eyes and just as tranquil. But he did not question that a Blackfoot Indian had ways of reading the sky that would elude most whites.

"How soon?" he asked.

"Tonight, maybe tomorrow. Soon."

"Then we better get a move on and find a good shelter for tonight's camp."

Blossom nodded quickly, pleased that Longarm was willing to act on her warning. As Longarm mounted up and watched Blossom and Andrea nag the unhappy Masters back into his saddle, he thought of Blossom's prediction and glanced skyward.

What next? he wondered.

He found out after they had bedded down for the night under the protection of a rock shelf. A hand raised his soogan's blanket. He glanced around and saw Andrea slipping in behind him.

He turned to face her. She grabbed his shoulders and pulled him against her, thrusting hungrily. "I need you," she said.

"I thought you'd had enough of that sort of thing," he said, kissing her lightly on her forehead and pulling her closer.

"You mean Masters?"

"Yes."

"That's one reason I want you. To get the stink of that man out of me."

"What's the other one?"

"I like you."

"We'll have to be quiet."

"Why? Let the son of a bitch hear us."

"I was thinking of Blossom."

She laughed. "Yes. But Indian women do not get jealous. And besides, you can have her tomorrow night. I will not protest."

"Nice of you," he said softly, leaning back so he could take her in.

He had almost forgotten how darkly ripe she was, breasts round, silken smooth, with little nipples that lay flat against dark circles. He let his eyes feast on her narrow waist, flaring hips, and the tiny belly that curved down to a dark, gleaming triangular nap. It was the generous flare of her hips that had first attracted him in Denver. They were beautifully molded, curving into thighs excitingly fleshy, legs long and slender. She had a thoroughly sensual body, and it was no wonder she had aroused the lust of Masters —and probably every man she had ever devoured with her dark, smoldering eyes.

It was quite a formidable weapon she had here, he re-

86

minded himself—one she used in the service of her people.

"You finished your inspection?" she asked huskily.

"Yes," he said.

She pulled him down to her. He kissed her, lips pressing her mouth open wider. He sent his tongue darting into her mouth, a messenger she welcomed. She pulled him down onto her breasts and he rubbed his mouth against them, glorying in their hot, lovely fragrance. He caught hold of one flat little pink nipple as it passed across his face, bit gently, yet hard enough to cause her to cry out.

He let his tongue circle the flat tip and felt it rise eagerly. He enclosed it gently, teasingly with his teeth. She gasped and her hands moved to tighten about his shoulders. He opened his mouth wider, sucked, pulled her breast up into his mouth, caressing it with his tongue.

Andrea cried out softly. Chuckling, he pushed himself atop her for a moment, and let his warm, throbbing organ press into her. Andrea's arms pulled more tightly about his neck as she thrust up at him, murmuring little sounds of pleasure. He shifted, moved from atop her. She cried out in protest, but the cry was cut off as his big hand began caressing first her breasts, then moving down across her rib cage, venturing over her little belly, plunging gently through the soft pubic hair, resting at last on the mound she now thrust eagerly up against his palm.

In an agony of need, Andrea's thighs moved together, then apart. He felt her nails raking feverishly up and down his back. He let his hand move past the moist lips and slip inside.

"Oh, Longarm," she murmured, the cry coming from deep in her throat. "Take me, please, I can't wait anymore!"

He brought his hand from her, pressed it into the soft

flesh of her inner thighs, pressed her legs wider apart, and saw her hips lift eagerly, begin to pump for him.

"Now!" she seethed, furious yet pleading. "Now!"

Her body lifted, shook, and she raked his back with her frenzied hands. He came over her, drove into her, and felt her tightness close around him. He drove deep, drew back, and drove in again, each thrust welcomed by her guttural gasps of pleasure. No sinuous writhings for Andrea. Hers was a total, enveloping physical absorption, every part of her body responding, her hot flesh beyond control. Suddenly her gasps halted. He felt her fingers dig cruelly into the backs of his legs.

Her muted cries rose, grew stronger, and then shattered. Her fingers dug still deeper into his legs and her body plunged upward, drew back, and slammed up against him, a scream exploding from her with the suddenness of a cougar's wail, piercing, almost ear-splitting, a shriek that held all the world's need inside it, hanging in the cold air, finally trailing away into little gasping sounds.

Longarm pulled back and smiled down at her.

"Oh, God," she moaned softly as she lay with her abdomen sucking in, then out, her body still responding involuntarily.

She turned in his arms as he finally drew away from her. Her hands reached up to pull his face down to hers, her lips found his mouth, soft, pliant lips.

Pulling gently back, he said teasingly, "I think maybe you woke up Blossom."

"I don't care," she breathed huskily.

"That sure was a lot more passion than I remember in Denver City."

"That was business in Denver. This was something entirely different. It was glorious. I'm glad this didn't happen

88

in Denver, Longarm. I don't think I would have been able to . . ."

"Betray me?"

She hesitated only a moment. "Yes," she whispered miserably.

He said softly, "I'm not finished yet. Do you mind?"

She laughed low, deliciously, and pulled him back up onto her. "Of course not. It's what I want, too."

Her pliant, eager lips enclosed his. Gently this time, he entered her. The wildness came again and drove him as it had her earlier. Soon they became two wild animals lost in each other, and when it came to an end at last, Longarm was ready for the deep, drugged sleep that took them both.

Chapter 8

According to Andrea, they were within a day's ride of Rock Lake. The temperature had been dropping steadily and a high, milky haze covered the sky. Grateful for his sheepskin coat, Longarm lifted its collar up around his neck and recalled Blossom's warning.

They were crossing a high ridge, a wooded mountain flank on their left, a steep ravine on their right. The drop was almost straight down, and gazing into the gorge, Longarm glimpsed the tracery of a mountain stream maybe a mile below him. Rapids showed as flecks of white against the stream's black sheen. Ahead of them a mountain's flank reared ominously. Behind them were the timbered slopes flanking the high pass through which they had just ridden.

The rifle shot came when they were halfway across the ridge. That was the signal. After it came the fusillade— from the trees behind them and from the timbered slope to their left. Keeping low, they spurred their horses along the ridge, heading for the wooded slope ahead of them. The whine of bullets filled the air. Rance's men—if that was who they were—appeared to be damn poor shots.

They had almost reached the pine-covered slope ahead of them when shots came at them from the pines. They had been encircled. This ridge had been a carefully planned trap. They had only one way to go: down the slope into the gorge. Longarm did not hesitate. He veered his horse and cut down the treacherous, shale-littered slope, heading for a ledge he glimpsed far below. He could see the tops of the pine trees that clothed it and he knew it would give them cover.

The others followed. Before they reached the ledge, however, they were forced to dismount and lead their horses carefully down the slippery shale and gravel. Longarm stayed behind with his rifle as the others guided their nervous horses lower. Masters was terrified. He stumbled after his horse, and Longarm thought he saw a devilish smile on Blossom's face as she noted the big Englishman's panic.

Longarm found a spot behind a clump of juniper and scanned the slope above him. Before long he caught sight of a hat inching down the steep incline toward him. Lifting his Winchester, Longarm sighted on the hat and waited. The hat got closer. Then it lifted and Longarm saw a be-whiskered face peering at him. He squeezed the trigger. The face exploded. A moment later a body hurtled past him down the slope and vanished into the abyss.

Below him the others had already reached the ledge and vanished into the pines. Longarm turned back around and waited for more of Rance's men to make their move. For a long while there was no sign of pursuit; then Longarm heard two men arguing. A moment later, off to his left, came the sound of gravel and shale being dislodged. He swung his rifle around just in time to catch two men emerging from behind a boulder. Working the Winchester's lever rapidly, Longarm cut down both men. They toppled backward down the slope, bounced once or twice, then vanished into the gorge.

Longarm waited for a good long while after that. But there were no more attempts by Rance's men to scramble down after them. It was close to sundown when he inched down the slope to the ledge. Blossom had already built a fire. Masters was pale from the dangerous descent, but Longarm could see the hope in his eyes. Standing near him, seething, was Andrea.

"We're trapped," she said. "We're trapped on this ledge."

"Maybe yes, maybe no."

"We got Masters for a hostage. I say we use him. Now."

"I was thinking the same thing."

"So what do we do? Just hand him over in exchange for our freedom?"

"If we could trust Rance and his men."

"I'd sooner trust the devil," she said.

"My feelings exactly."

"So what do we do?"

"All we really need is a delay. Something to distract them, keep them here while we move off."

Longarm glanced back along the ledge. On the way down the slope, he had noticed a narrow game trail leading off the ledge and disappearing into a cleft in the mountainside. Beyond the cleft he had seen a thick carpet of pine covering a farther, more gentle slope out of the gorge. Their escape lay that way—if they could delay Rance and his men long enough.

Longarm loosed the rope from his saddle and advanced on Masters. One look at the rope and Masters went white.

"What're you going to do?" he cried.

"Put you on display. Attract attention. What we need is a diversion, and it looks like you're it."

Longarm shook open the loop, then dropped it over Masters's shoulders, tightening it quickly as soon as it reached his upper arms. Then he stepped closer and wound the rope three times around his upper torso, then knotted it so the rope would not ride up past the man's shoulders.

"What are you going to do, Longarm?" Andrea asked.

"Give this fellow here a chance to scream like a stuck pig. He's sure to draw a crowd like that."

"Speak plain."

"Watch."

Longarm turned Masters around, then kicked him gently forward, toward the lip of the ledge on which they were standing. He yelped in terror. Snugging the rope around a thin pine, Longarm pushed him again. Masters screamed and toppled off the ledge. Longarm braced himself. The rope snapped taut. Edging toward the lip of the ledge, Longarm looked down. Masters, swinging over the abyss at the end of the rope, was still screaming.

"Rance!" he was yelling. "Get me up! Get me up!"

Longarm lowered him still further until he was swinging just above the tops of the trees on the slope below. Far below the trees, the stream was still only a distant black ribbon coiling through the gorge. The white water seemed a little closer, but Longarm still could not hear it from this height.

Moving back carefully along the rope, Longarm wrapped it securely around the pine, then knotted it.

"Now what?" asked Andrea, her dark eyes gleaming

with pleasure. The sound of Masters's screaming was music to her ears.

"We'll let him hang there for a while," Longarm told her. "The racket he's making should draw Rance and his men. I'll be over there in those rocks, keeping them from the ledge. That should give you and Blossom enough time to get over that game trail and onto the far slope. I'll follow as soon as I get the chance."

"You sure they won't track us?"

"As sure as I can be. The way I figure it, once Masters gets lifted out of that gorge, all he's going to want to do is to return to his place to recover."

"Why gamble? Why not make damn sure he goes back with his men?"

"How do you propose we do that?"

"Hurt him bad enough."

"What do you mean?"

"I'll show you," she said. A knife materialized in her hand and she started over to the rope.

He strode quickly over and stopped her. "For God's sake, Andrea. Cut that rope and you might kill him."

"What difference would that make? Rance and his men would not know for sure if he was dead. They'd have to go down there to find him. You wouldn't have to hold them to give us a chance to escape, and we'd be rid of this bastard once and for all."

"It would be murder."

"You think that would stop him? This is war."

"It's not my war."

He grabbed her wrist and twisted. The knife dropped from her grasp. She flared at him angrily, her eyes blazing. "Damn you, Longarm! You got no right to protect that bastard!"

"I am not protecting him," Longarm told her patiently.

95

"I'm thinking of us—you and Blossom. Do as I say, will you? Go with Blossom down that trail."

She spun about and mounted up. Longarm handed her knife back up to her. She took it and, without a word, spurred her horse on through the pines. Blossom grabbed the reins of her pack horse and scrambled Indian-style onto her mount, then booted her horse after Andrea. As the Indian girl left the pines, she glanced back at him, obviously worried.

Leading his horse, Longarm hurried after them until he came to the huge pile of rocks he had noticed jutting out above the game trail. Tethering his horse beyond them, he climbed up into the rocks and found himself a comfortable perch between a boulder and a gnarled juniper tree. The juniper's roots clutched at the side of the gorge like the fingers of a powerful hand. He was counting on the juniper's trunk to keep him from toppling into the gorge if he took a round.

He checked the load in his Winchester, then his Colt. Satisfied, he scanned the nearly sheer slope above him. He could clearly hear Masters's piercing screams and cries for help. He had expected them to diminish some by this time, but they still reverberated loudly throughout the gorge, a haunting, terrifying series of screeches and cries for help that filled the air with sheer terror.

The first of Masters's men to appear on the slope was Karl. Longarm took aim, fired, and saw the ground kick up just in front of him. Karl scrambled hastily back up the slope. No one else tried to reach the ledge for at least fifteen minutes. Then two men exploded onto the ledge, found cover behind some pines, and began peppering the rocks where Longarm crouched. Longarm waited patiently, his finger resting lightly on the Winchester's trigger, as he rested his sights on the tree one of the men was crouched

96

behind. The fellow leaned out to peer at the rocks. Longarm rested his sight on the man's chest and caressed the trigger. The stock bit into his shoulder and the fellow exploded back, disappearing. The other one darted from the trees and vanished up the slope.

Complete darkness fell not long after. The cloud cover had thickened along with the chill and there were no stars, no moon. In the deepening gloom of the gorge, Masters's pitiable cries were growing fainter with each passing second. Perhaps it was time for Longarm to mount up and follow Andrea and Blossom up the game trail.

Longarm heard a stealthy footfall behind him. He started to turn. What felt like the side of a mountain fell on his head. He grabbed for the tree he had been resting against, missed, and toppled backward through space. He came down hard on one shoulder, cartwheeled through space for an instant or so, then slammed against a boulder. He hung there for a moment, his entire side numb. Instinctively, he groped out and grabbed hold of some brush. It began to pull free of the slope. He reached out with his other hand and this time caught hold of a pine tree's roots.

With both hands he clung to them while the cold, dark universe wheeled about him. The blow on his head had opened his scalp. Blood was seeping down his forehead and the side of his face, but he could do nothing until his senses cleared.

Then, dimly, he heard light running footsteps above him crossing to the ledge. A moment later Masters's interminable wailing rose to a sudden, horrified shriek. It lasted a long moment, grew fainter, then ended abruptly. The light footsteps above Longarm came again, this time racing back off the ledge. In a moment they had disappeared up the game trail.

Longarm clung to the pine's roots, his senses continuing

to reel sickeningly. Twice he almost passed out. He could hear Rance's men scrambling back up the slope. Not long after he heard cries from the gorge below. Then came the distant echo of shouts and the clatter of horses, this time coming from the gorge far below him.

Longarm knew exactly what had happened. Andrea had cut the rope, sending the man she loathed crashing through the trees to the bottom of the gorge. And it had done the trick. Rance's men were no longer a problem for them. To accomplish this, Andrea had been quite willing to send Longarm to his death.

Longarm smiled. That was how much a woman's passion was worth.

Once his senses returned to normal, Longarm attempted to pull himself back up the steep slope, but his way was blocked by a sheer wall of rock. He would have to be a fly in order to traverse the slick granite brow that bent out over him. He tried to work his way down the cliff, but found only cold emptiness beneath his swinging, probing feet. He hauled himself back up to the pine tree and wondered how long he could hold out. Already the cold was having its effect on him. A chill was seeping into his bones and he felt a weakness stealing over him, robbing his hands of the strength he needed to hold on to his precarious perch.

"Longarm!"

It was Blossom's voice. She was back on the ledge. From where he was, he could not see her.

"Over here!"

He did not hear a thing then until a few moments later. She called to him again, this time from almost directly overhead.

"Down here," he called.

He heard nothing until a thin avalanche of gravel sluiced down past him. He looked up, squinting. A rope snaked out of the night and fell past him. He reached out with one hand and grabbed it. He tugged on it twice. Blossom let it out a little. He tugged one more time, and she let it out still more. As swiftly as he could, he tied the rope around his chest under his armpits, knotted it securely, then tugged once, sharply, on the rope.

"Haul me up!"

The rope went taut. He tested it, then swung out, bracing himself against the rock face. Slowly he worked his way up the side of the rock. His right thigh had been banged up some and any exertion on it caused considerable pain, but he did not allow this to slow him. He continued to climb back up, pulled himself over the rocky brow, then moved on up the remaining slope. The rope was a real help to him.

When he reached the game trail where Blossom was waiting, he glanced down, startled to see how far he had plunged. Blossom had snubbed the rope around a pine and used his horse to keep the rope taut. He untied the rope from around his waist, then hurried back up into the rocks for his Winchester and Colt. He found the Colt on the ground beside his hat, close to where he had been struck from behind. The Winchester was lying on the game trail below the rocks. He returned to his horse and dropped the rifle into the scabbard.

Then he looked at her. By coming back for him, she had saved his life. He could not have lasted much longer clinging to that pine.

"You want to tell me what happened, Blossom?"

She nodded. "Andrea, she say she go back to see why you not come. But when she come back without you, I ask her what happened. She tell me you dead and then she ride on past me. I try to stop her, but she knock me from my horse. Then I know it is bad for you."

"If you thought I was dead, why did you come back?"

"You very big man. I think maybe it not so easy to kill you."

"Thanks, Blossom."

She shrugged. "We go now?"

"Yeah. Let's get a move on. It's getting pretty damn chilly up here."

An hour or so later, his thigh and shoulder were giving him considerable trouble. Blossom pointed to a trail moving up into the timber, well off the route they were taking.

"Up there," she said, pointing, "is trapper's cabin. I live there once."

"Where's the trapper?"

"Grizzly take him."

"Lead the way."

She turned her horse, the pack horse following, and in less than an hour they were moving out onto a high meadow, on the far edge of which he glimpsed the cabin. It was built into the side of the mountain. When they got to it, Longarm saw the door hanging open on its leather hinges, and the windows, all two of them, gaping open. But there were wooden shutters on the inside and it still had a solid roof and sides.

Blossom went inside first. She returned after a quick inspection and helped him down from his horse.

"It is not so good in there," she told him. "But it will soon be much worse out here. Better we go inside now."

Longarm, in pain with each step he took, his shoulder and right thigh throbbing painfully, hobbled into the cabin. Blossom opened his bedroll. He kicked off his boots and crawled into it. Blossom vanished outside to take care of the horses. When she returned, Longarm was almost asleep.

He was dimly aware of her slipping into the soogan with him. The warmth of her body was like a blessing. His shivering ceased and almost at once he fell into a deep, dreamless sleep.

He awoke the next morning to the sound of a demented wind. Snow had sifted in through cracks in the shuttered windows and under the door. Blossom had gone. He threw aside his soogan and got to his feet. The cold was so intense his entire body was shivering, and he had difficulty keeping his teeth from chattering out of control. He went to the door, amazed at how difficult it was for him to move. Every bone and every muscle in his body protested.

A drift had propped the door shut. He struggled grimly with it and finally pushed it open. As soon as he did, a blast of frigid air rushed into the cabin, a swirl of driving snow coming with it. He peered outside. Overnight the world had been transformed. A driving curtain of snow all but obliterated the line of timber close by the cabin. Then, out of the swirling snow, Blossom appeared, carrying firewood she must have dug out of the wooded slope above the cabin.

She brushed in past him, smelling of snow, her cheeks aflame from the wind. He helped her build a fire in the fireplace and was grateful to see how well it drew. While she built up the fire, Longarm busied himself blocking out the cracks in the window shutters. Before long the fire crackling in the fireplace had the cabin surprisingly warm.

Then, despite his protests, Blossom went out for more firewood.

Longarm had taken a nasty plunge, landing first on his shoulder, then wrapping himself around a boulder before managing to grab hold of that pine. Not until the shock of it wore off much later did he realize how much he had been punished. Though he had broken no bones, a lot of his hinges were strained mightily, and a few bolts had almost worked loose. In the days that followed, he found he could barely move—and when he did, he wished he hadn't.

Blossom saw his difficulty and massaged his aching body whenever he seemed to need it. She kept the laceration on his scalp clean and before long, his hair grew over the spot. For the most part, however, she let him rest, and at night her warm body pressed close against his did much to hasten his recovery.

She had tethered the horses in a sheltering grove of trees behind the cabin. The provisions she had taken from Masters's larder were more than sufficient to last them for a week. There was no need to panic, therefore, as the snow continued to fall, the drifts growing higher with each passing hour. Indeed, as the snow piled up about the cabin, the howl of the wind grew more distant, restful even, the firewood crackling in the fireplace a pleasant, lulling sound.

Using Longarm's pocketknife, Blossom had carved a pipe for him out of a piece of dried wood during the second day of the blizzard. Then she had found him some sweet bark to smoke in it. While she had worked on the pipe, she had hummed an Indian tune softly to herself. Now, feeling much better as he stood by the window and puffed contentedly on his pipe, he found himself humming the same tune.

Blossom finished building up the fire and walked over to peer with him out through a crack at the storm. It seemed to be blowing just as fiercely as before.

She looked up at him. "Is your leg better now?"

"Much better."

"And your shoulder?"

"It's fine."

"Maybe it hurt a little. Maybe I better rub it for you again."

He was about to tell her it was not necessary, but thought better of it when he saw the hunger in her eyes.

"All right," he said.

Her eyes gleaming, she took his hand and led him over to his soogan. Until now, though she had slept with him in order to keep them both warm, she had made no effort to seduce him, and he had been scrupulous in making no moves toward her. It was not just the severe pain in his thigh and the deep ache in his shoulder, but the memory of Andrea and the fact of her betrayal. It had left him a trifle sour.

But he realized now what a damn fool reason that was to hold back from Blossom. He pulled her down beside him on the soogan.

Chapter 9

Alone with this quiet, efficient Blackfoot woman, Long-arm was willing to admit to himself that he had found—at least for now—a peace and contentment that had long eluded him. He did not mind the storm's demented howl, or the long twilit days he spent with her in the trapper's cabin. Time stood still for them. Not only his body but his spirit began to heal. The mile-high city and its smoke-filled saloons and gaming rooms, the bark of shouting, drunken men punctuated by the shrill laughter of bought women— all that faded, became part of another existence, a distant, unpleasant world to which he was in no hurry to return.

He had been sent up here to bring back a bank robber in handcuffs and if possible to regain the fortune in silver certificates the robber and his gang had taken from a Wisconsin bank. In reality, however, Longarm was part of those malign forces arrayed against the leaders of a doomed separatist movement. It was a dirty business.

Longarm did not like his part in it, even though, as far as he could see, Dupre and the other Meti leaders could not possibly prevail against the government in Ottawa.

Nor was there any chance that their cause might generate sympathy where it counted. The Metis were, after all, half-breeds, a despised mix of Indian and white blood, worthy only of contempt from the more favored English settlers whose bloodlines were uncontaminated. This invincible arrogance made it possible for them to commit any atrocity with impunity. They were the chosen; the Metis were the despised. The world belonged to the pure in blood.

For their part, the Metis could do no less than to fight back with the cruel tenacity of any people whose life and livelihood were about to be ripped from them without compensation.

And Longarm found himself squarely in the middle.

It was no wonder he preferred the company of the quiet Blackfoot woman and the isolating storm that closed them off from that other world.

One morning they awoke to a silent world, a prodigious silence, unearthly and frightening. Longarm got up and pulled open the door. Out of a bright blue, cloudless sky the sun was pouring forth in all its glory. The dazzling brightness of it stabbed into his eyes. He glanced quickly away. Beside him, Blossom peered out, one hand held up before her eyes while she peered through the cracks between her fingers.

It was cold—a numbing, intense cold that caused them to pull the door shut quickly and hurry over to the fireplace. The coals were still glowing. Swiftly they built a roaring fire. Then, in minutes, Blossom had coffee for him, and not long after sourdough biscuits and the last of the beans.

The storm, he realized, had blown over just in time. He would have to leave this snug retreat and do some hunting. Despite the cold, it was a prospect he found himself looking forward to.

"We need fresh meat," he told her.

She nodded. "Yes."

He dressed as warmly as he could while she packed what food he would need and wrapped it in his bedroll.

"You say there's grizzly around here?" he asked, as he took the bedroll from her and placed it near the door.

"Many grizzly. Be careful."

"I will," he said, shrugging into his sheepskin and picking up his rifle. He checked its load, then dropped a box of cartridges into one of his pockets. He dropped his Colt into his holster and examined the cutting edge of the bowie he had taken from Masters's place. One thing he wished he had was a pair of gloves. He would be at a distinct disadvantage without them.

As he started for the door, Blossom said, "Wait, please."

He turned to see her pulling from under her neat pile of clothing a pair of gloves. They were newly made from buckskin. Then he remembered. She had worked for half a day on them, though at the time Longarm had thought she was just mending one of her skirts.

He took them from her. "Thanks," he said, pulling them on.

"You must keep sun from your eyes," she told him.

"You got any ideas?"

"Tie two sticks together with rawhide. Look at world between them."

Longarm grinned at her. He recalled seeing some Blackfoot Indians wearing such improvised sunshades after a blizzard a few years before. At the time he had been

107

impressed at their utility. Snow blindness could be devastating in a world altered so completely by snow piled into drifts six to ten feet high.

"I will be back with fresh meat," he said, picking up his bedroll. "It might take a few days."

"I will wait here," she told him calmly.

He turned and pushed out into the white, sparkling world.

Hunting men was a damn sight easier than hunting wild game.

Longarm led the pack horse through drift after drift, over a landscape bright with sunlight and barren of any sign of life. Not even a hawk or an eagle crossed the sky. From the dark folds of timber enclosing the bluffs and hogbacks all around him, there did not issue a single bird call.

He had told Blossom it might take him a few days, but at the close of the third day, no longer so confident of his abilities as a hunter of red meat, he decided that on the morrow it would be wise for him to circle back to the cabin, with or without fresh game. It was a decision he made reluctantly, but without snowshoes, the going had been incredibly difficult. The horse was about done in, as well. Fortunately, Blossom had thought to pack grain for the animal along with the coffee and sourdough she had given him.

He camped that night in a thicket beside a frozen stream. The thought that on the next day he would be on his way back to the cabin lulled him. He closed his eyes and sleep smote him like a fist. When he awoke the next morning, he was aware of a gentle but persistent pressure on his back and shoulders. He tried to turn over. To his astonishment, he found he was almost completely buried by a fresh blanket of snow at least two feet deep. He poked his arm through the snow cover, then pushed back his soogan and struggled to a sitting position. The snow was still falling, coming down so heavily it seemed as if someone were shaking feathers out of a giant pillow just over his head.

He had a difficult time retrieving his soogan and the rest of his camp gear from this additional snowfall. The pack horse had drifted off. He found it in a small ravine, the snow reaching clear to its belly. The animal was in a mild panic and Longarm hurried to trample the snow down around it, then led the horse from the ravine. He remembered that he had been moving along below a ridge the day before. Peering up through the snow, he tried to spot it again. On higher ground, he hoped, where the wind had a chance to sweep the snow clear, it might not be as deep. Already the wind was picking up, blinding him momentarily as it flung great stinging sheets of snow at him. Finally he glimpsed the ridge ahead of him and pushed toward it through the hip-deep snow.

Sighting it was one thing. Reaching it was something else again. He struggled through ever-deepening drifts; it took him most of the morning to pull himself and the horse up onto the ridge. By the time he had done so, he was almost totally exhausted, as was the pack horse. As he had hoped, the drifts were not so deep on the ridge, but the wind now cut at him with numbing force. He kept on, however, until he found a shallow cavern in the face of the rock wall, its entrance partially blocked off by juniper bushes and an upthrusting finger of rock. He led the horse into the cavern, then slumped wearily down himself.

He did not allow himself to rest for long. He was soaked clean through and his feet were tingling dangerously. In the rear of the depression he found a few dry pine boughs and managed to get a fire going. Once it was going well enough, he was able to feed it larger branches and chunks of wood he dug out from under the first snowfall. Soon he had a roaring fire. The horse came closer and seemed as pleased and grateful for the warmth as Longarm was.

By nightfall he had fashioned himself an effective shelter from the wind and snow and was cozy enough. There was enough dry firewood to keep the fire going through the night and well into the next day. If used sparingly, he had enough grain to last the horse for a few more days, at least. He had not expected another snowfall so hard upon the first, but unlike the first storm, this one had overtaken him on cat feet. But the cat feet were gone now. The wind in its belly was rising, its howl rising to a shriek as night fell.

Two days later the snow let up, and with it the wind. There had been no cabin to muffle its cry this time, and its constant moan had entered his soul, shriveling it. But the chill that came with the clear blue sky was almost as intimidating. Again the world was clean of color, except white and the black stand of pine clothing the ridges and mountainsides.

His supply of sourdough biscuits and his sack of beans was gone by this time. There was not even any coffee, and the horse had eaten the last of the grain the night before. There was no room for bad luck now. He had to shoot himself some fresh meat, or the weakness that would overtake his limbs would make it impossible for him to return to the cabin.

He checked his Winchester and Colt, left the horse behind, and trudged out from the cavern's shelter and started along the ridge. Following it for more than a mile, he caught sight of a small pack of wolves in the meadow below. They appeared to be following the track of some game—elk perhaps, or deer. He moved down off the ridge. Almost at once, however, he found the snowdrifts so deep he could barely struggle through them. By the time he reached the spot where he had last seen the wolves, the landscape was as empty as before.

It was midafternoon by this time. Already the cold was settling in, a chilling drop that crept with insidious persistence into the marrow of his bones. He stamped his feet continually to keep the circulation going and thanked Blossom over and over for the deerskin gloves that kept his hands from freezing.

Reluctantly, he turned back to the cavern. There might be a better chance to find game on the ridge, where the snow was not so deep, and the hoofed deer could find graze. On the way back, he made better time, since he had already bulled something approaching a path through the snow. He was moving into the sun now and at this quickened pace, the racing blood warmed him agreeably. He was even beginning to sweat some. Feeling more hopeful, he moved now as patiently as an animal, trudging without thought, feeling the sun's warmth, his nostrils quivering to the sharp, spicy tang of the firs and his mind pleasantly aware of the massive, hulking mountains shouldering against the blue sky on all sides of him.

But as he approached the cavern, he sensed trouble. He came alert instantly. Crouching, he moved toward a massive, triangular rock jutting out of the snow-covered ground. Reaching it, he poked his head around it. Ahead of him, at a distance of two hundred yards or so, was the dark socket of the cavern. He frowned. He had expected to see the pack horse either standing in the entrance or out on the ridge, pawing hopefully for some forage. He moved out from behind the boulder and advanced cautiously.

Almost immediately, he found himself on higher

ground—just high enough to see into a depression beside the cavern. He stiffened. The pack horse was not visible, but something else was—a large animal, something low and ominous. Puzzled, Longarm peered more closely at the dark shape. It was working over something. He moved closer until he caught the dark glass of a claw bright with blood as it slashed down into something half-buried in the snow.

Longarm swore, then dropped quickly back behind the boulder. Moving as swiftly as he could in the deep snow, he worked his way around to the other side of the ridge, where there was pine cover closer to the cavern's entrance. As he moved, he kept just below the ridge's rim. He regained the ridge a few feet from the pine. Then, using the stand for cover, he worked his way closer to the cavern entrance—and what was left of his pack horse.

There was no doubt in Longarm's mind by now. It was a grizzly he had seen feeding on the pack horse, its silver hump ducking and rising as it ripped and tore at the horse's flesh. Slipping steadily closer through the pines, Longarm was soon close enough to see raw entrails of the horse spewed out over the snow, the snow beneath its ruined carcass trampled into red slush. Longarm stepped out of cover and raised his Winchester.

The grizzly lifted its enormous bulk and spun to face Longarm, its bloody muzzle steaming from the hot entrails it had been devouring. The bear was a male and stood a full eight feet tall. Longarm did not wait. He aimed carefully and squeezed off a round in one swift, fluid motion. The round thunked into the great animal's powerful chest.

He staggered slightly, then caught himself, and with a roar, charged. His gait was lumbering and the snow was deep, yet he covered the distance between the horse and

Longarm with astonishing speed. Longarm levered swiftly and fired twice more, punching one more hole in the chest, and another one in the side of his snout. Bone and bloody gristle exploded from the shattered snout, but this did not slow the bear at all.

Longarm levered and fired once more, then ducked back into the pines. The bear crashed blindly into the brush and swept past him, then caught himself and spun around, his tiny red eyes fixing on Longarm. By this time Longarm had his Colt out. Flinging off his gloves, he fired twice into the dark mass of blood that was the grizzly's chest. Infuriated, the bear rose to his full height and let out a shattering roar.

Trampling a large juniper bush underfoot, the bear charged. Longarm back up hastily, emptying his Colt into the bear. His last shot passed through the shattered mouth and into the great beast's brain. The bear stopped less than a foot from Longarm, took a wild swipe at him, then collapsed face down in the snow.

Longarm stood for a moment, panting slightly, the smoking Colt in his hand, looking down at the magnificent beast sprawled in the bloody snow at his feet. He was waiting for the beast to move, rear up perhaps, and come at him again.

At last he was ready to believe it. The bear was dead.

Longarm had gone far looking for fresh meat. It had been here all the time, waiting for him: horsemeat.

The problem Longarm faced now was transporting back to the cabin that portion of the horse's rear haunch that had not been devoured by the bear. He studied its size and decided he would have to construct a sled to pull it on. He set to work at once. Cutting the saplings with his bowie and tying them together with vines into a crude but serviceable sledge was a slow, tedious job, hampered by the deep drifts and the cruel cold. By the time he had finished, the sun was resting on the horizon and it was considerably colder. Longarm decided to wait until the next day before setting out.

He lashed the entire haunch and a good portion of the right foreleg to the sled, then pulled it after him into the cavern. He was pleased at how easily the sled negotiated the snow. The rest of the daylight he used to gather a sufficient supply of firewood and build up the fire.

Dusk was falling when Longarm first heard the wolves. He swore at his stupidity, left the cavern, and dragged the remains of the horse away from the cavern and into the pines, dropping them alongside the bear's carcass. It was already snowing lightly when he got back to the cavern. Before long the night was a luminous, ghostly white as the snow sifted straight down. He could hear the snow falling, a faint, eerie sound.

Not much later he could hear the wolves prowling nearby. They were much closer now. Their high-pitched, barking yelps lifted the hair on the back of his neck. Before long they were into the pines, feeding on the bear and the remains of the pack horse.

He caught the gleam of eyes staring into the cavern at him and promptly piled more wood on his fire. As the flames leaped higher, the eyes winked out, but the wolves did not go away. They could smell the haunch and foreleg resting on his sled. Not until midnight did the growling and snapping that accompanied the wolves' feasting diminish and the gleaming eyes vanish into the snowfall.

For three more days the snow fell. On the fourth day, the snow stopped sometime before dawn. A feeble sun peered down at an alabaster world through a pale sky. Longarm was nearly crazy from being pent up in the cavern. He would have welcomed it if the wolves had returned during those long nights. But they had vanished into the mists of snow, leaving him to his chill solitude.

Attaching the horse's reins to the sled, he set out at once. The additional snowfall meant he was now plowing through drifts that sometimes reached clear up to his waist and even higher. Sweat poured off him as he labored. His eyebrows and the hair on the back of his neck grew heavy with frozen perspiration.

Coming out onto a wide parkland by midafternoon, he started across its pristine, unmarked surface. Halfway across he noticed distant moving patches on the horizon, off to his left. The patches became distinct and recognizable before long as they leaped toward him through the snow, tongues lolling, tails up.

Longarm counted eight wolves in all.

Whether it was the same pack that had finished off the bear and the horse's remains, he did not know. In the upholstered confines of Denver drawing rooms, Longarm had been told by experts in such matters that any tales of wolves attacking trappers and lone hunters was utter nonsense. Wolves, these polished gents had assured him, would never attack a man; they avoided man whenever possible and were always anxious to give him a wide berth. But as Longarm watched this particular pack of wolves plunging toward him through the snow, it occurred to him that maybe these particular wolves hadn't yet got the message.

Like Longarm, they found themselves in a world where all the familiar landmarks had been obliterated by an impenetrable cover of snow. The small game they might have been able to feed on had burrowed safely out of sight beneath it, while the bigger game was sheltered in the timber, busy pawing through the drifts to get at graze, leaving no fresh scents or tracks for the wolves to follow.

Apart from themselves and maybe a few birds, Longarm

must have been the first living creature they had glimpsed since the first snowfall more than a week ago. And wolves were bright enough to realize that what lived and moved contained flesh, blood, and sinew. They were probably already slavering as they drew close enough to see him—and the raw chunks of frozen meat he was pulling behind him on the sled.

The wolves started to string out in a long line that ran parallel to Longarm's course. They were still on his left. He estimated that they were about three hundred yards distant. It was almost as if they knew precisely the range of Longarm's Winchester and were keeping just beyond it. Plumes of snow erupted before them each time their plunging forepaws came down. Their pace was steady, relentless. Longarm could not help marveling at their prodigious energy, and at the hunger that must be building inside them with each stride.

Longarm decided he had better find a shelter so he could build a fire big enough to intimidate this unsettling wolf pack. A few minutes later he sighted a ridge a mile or so in the distance. Above it was a sheer mountain wall so steep that portions of its face were entirely clear of snow.

He headed for the ridge, certain he would be able to find shelter in those rocks above it, more than likely a cave of some kind. Once he found such a shelter, he would be able to build a fire.

He kept on pulling toward the distant ridge, his shoulders raw from the ceaseless rubbing of the reins. When he was close enough, he held up and studied the ridge carefully, hoping for sign of a cave. Almost immediately he was rewarded. The cavern was quite large, a towering ponderosa pine standing like a sentinel outside its entrance. A fire at its entrance would easily keep off the wolves. But though the slope leading up to the ridge seemed an easy enough trek for him, there was a long stand of timber running along the base of the ridge. He would have to go through that in order to reach the ridge, and once he ventured into that timber, the wolves would close in.

Yet, if he stayed out here on the flat, when night came the wolves would simply encircle him and wait. With no firewood to build a fire, he would either be torn apart by the famished pack or he would freeze to death. He had no alternative. The ridge was his only hope.

He started for the timber.

Chapter 10

The wolves were still strung out on his left when Longarm reached the timber. He plunged into it and at once had trouble with the sled. It was continually getting caught by bushes or slamming into trees. Longarm shortened the reins and turned about to guide it more carefully. This meant he was forced to slow down considerably.

By the time he made it through the timber and started up the slope to the ridge, the wolves had penetrated the timber also and were now much closer to him. Hauling the sled up the slope through the drifts was more difficult than he had imagined it would be. Two of the nearest wolves sat down abruptly in the snow, their tails curled around them, and watched him struggle. No sense in them getting all worn out, it seemed. They would let Longarm do the hauling for them. It was a crazy, comical thought, and it came to Longarm at a time when he was beginning to realize how tenacious the wolves were going to be. They had no intention of letting him get away from them, not while Longarm was still hauling the frozen carcass.

Longarm reached the ridge and started along it toward the cave he had spotted. Before long he saw his mistake. What had looked like a gaping hole in the cliffside from the flat below was merely a depression in a huge snow bank, one hollowed out by swirling winds.

There would be no shelter for him on this ridge.

He kept going, the wolves moving past him to the cliff-side, then keeping pace with him as he moved down the ridge. They kept a judicious distance from him, respecting the fact that he might have a firearm that could reach out and punish them. The ridge became a long butte as the cliff fell away to be replaced with a steep mountainside carpeted with thick timber. The wolves remained between him and the timber.

Before long the timber—and the wolves—were crowding him on his right, pushing him to the left, toward the edge of the butte. A few wolves, their snouts low to the snow, their eyes on him every second, crossed and re-crossed in front of him, some even settling in the snow, their snouts resting on their paws as he passed less than a hundred yards from them. Longarm could see in their eyes and in their movements that they were getting bolder, more confident.

He crested a slight ridge and saw a thick stand of pine ahead of him, marching straight across the butte to its edge. Beyond the timber he saw rough country, great boulders piled high, sheer rock faces. The shelter he sought was most likely in there, but once again he would have to go through a stretch of timber with the wolf pack, much bolder now, still on his heels.

The timber began to crowd him. The wolves were already moving through it. They were keeping pace with him still. He caught glimpses of them as they flitted silently through the timber like gray ghosts. He intended to keep out of the pine forest for as long as he possibly could, but this forced him to move along the edge of the butte, a dangerous course.

During the first snowfall, the wind had carved great, sweeping ridges that extended out over the edge of the butte. He noticed the earlier frozen banks of snow sticking out occasionally from under the later, fresher snow. The later snowfalls had evidently buried the first ridges, lending an air of solidity to the frozen embankment it did not really possess. Twice he felt the snow shift under his weight as the underside of the frozen snow bank dropped lower.

At last he abandoned the precarious snow bank and started through the pine timber. Almost at once he became aware of a large gray wolf less than ten yards from him, tongue lolling, eyes gleaming in the forest gloom. Other wolves appeared. They were closer to him and bolder, as if they felt that once he had entered their domain, he was no longer capable of harming them. They did not bark or howl or snarl. And before long, that in itself became unnerving. Glancing back, he saw wolves trotting silently after him, their paws coming down onto the path his sled was making.

Ahead of him he saw the pines thinning. Beyond the pines were the rocks and a possible shelter—and safety from his silent companions. He increased his speed, and at once the sled snagged on a gnarled juniper tree whose branches were barely visible above the snow. He dropped the reins, turned, and trudged quickly back to release it, his Winchester held at the ready. He pulled the sled loose, then turned around.

Two of the largest wolves he had ever seen were sitting

on the reins, watching him alertly, almost as if they were waiting for him to initiate a game of fetch. He felt the hair on the back of his neck prickle. He knew he was not going to be able to keep going with this sled unless he killed those two wolves.

He raised his rifle. The two wolves charged. He got off a shot that took the head off the closest wolf, but before he could lever a fresh cartridge into the firing chamber, the second wolf struck him in the chest. Longarm went down so fast that the wolf tumbled past him, landing in a deep drift. Longarm spun about and braced himself as the wolf charged back at him. Using his rifle as a club, he slammed the wolf hard on the side of the head. The wolf went tumbling head over heels into the brush, yelping.

A low chorus of growls came from behind him. He turned. Three wolves were charging at him out of the pines. Drawing his Colt, Longarm snapped off one useless shot before the wolves bowled him over. He felt heavy paws on his chest and hot breath on his face as the two wolves bolted past him and lunged at the frozen carcass tied to the sled. Jumping to his feet, Longarm grabbed up his rifle, then the reins attached to the sled. Yanking it around, he pulled it away from the wolves, turned, and dragged it as fast as he could out of the timber onto the snow ridge.

Suddenly the ground gave away beneath him as the entire ridge of snow collapsed under his weight and that of the sled. Enveloped in a shower of snow, he tumbled through space. He was aware of cold air slicing into his lungs as he flipped completely around, then plowed, shoulder first, into a snow bank so deep that he and the sled were almost completely buried.

The wolves landed in a snowdrift not too far from him. He struggled to his feet. Three wolves were floundering in the deep drift. Longarm pulled his Colt, aimed at the closest one, and fired. The gun misfired. He cocked and fired again. Nothing. The snow had fouled the powder. He caught sight of the barrel of his Winchester poking out of the snow. He snatched it up and lunged toward the wolf.

The snow made it difficult for him to swing the rifle barrel. His first blow only glanced off the wolf's head, stunning it. Steadying himself in the deep snow as best he could, he swung a second time and crushed the wolf's skull. The other two wolves, still unable to gain a firm foothold in the drift, waited with bared fangs for Longarm to reach them. As he approached, they crouched low, uttering deep, guttural growls. But they were no longer attacking, Longarm realized. They were simply standing their ground. In the manner of wolves, they were willing to accept a standoff.

And that seemed like a damn good idea to Longarm.

He turned back to the sled and righted it. He heard a wolf's startled yelp from the ridge. Glancing up, he saw four wolves in the midst of a small avalanche, tumbling headlong into space. Landing in a great shower of snow about fifty yards from Longarm, they righted themselves and began leaping and struggling through the deep snow toward the other two wolves. On the ridge, three more wolves appeared—then two more.

Longarm would have to compromise.

With his bowie, he cut through the vines he had used to tie the meat to the sled, then tossed the horse's foreleg into a deep drift some distance from him. It wasn't much, but it might give him the time he needed to gain the rocks ahead. While the wolves struggled eagerly through the snow toward the meat, he bound the remaining haunch to the sled and moved off quickly.

A few minutes later, as he hauled the lighter sled up out

of the ravine, he looked back down and saw the wolves tearing into the meat like sharks into a dead whale.

Two days later, Longarm peered anxiously down at the cabin. There was no sign of Blossom. No smoke was pulsing from the fireplace chimney, and in front of the cabin the bodies of two men were sprawled in the snow.

Earlier, he had noted patches of trampled snow in the flat below the cabin caused by milling horsemen. Moving closer to the cabin, he had glimpsed the two dead men, their bodies partially covered by a recent light snowfall. That was when he decided to hide the sled in the pines and approach the cabin from the rear.

He levered a fresh cartridge into the Winchester's firing chamber and started down the slope toward the cabin.

"Hold it right there, mister!"

The command came from a stand of timber off to his right. Longarm froze.

A tall man dressed in the traditional garb of a trapper stepped out of the trees, a Sharps rifle in his hands. His face was almost entirely hidden behind a thick blond beard. The angry look in his eyes was accentuated by their fierce, light blue intensity.

"Who the hell are you?" Longarm demanded.

"Franklin Adams. Now you know that, what good does it do you, English?"

The trapper was not a Meti, that was for sure. He spoke English with a clipped Eastern accent—and he spoke it well.

"I am not English," Longarm told him.

"You got a name?"

"Ned Barker. What happened here?"

"A large body of riders—Canadians—was what I saw.

They acted like vigilantes. They were led by a tall Englishman."

It was what Longarm had feared from the moment he saw the trampled snow below the cabin. "I left a woman down there. Where is she?"

"A woman?"

"Yes, a young Blackfoot woman."

"She have a name?" The trapper's voice had softened a bit.

"Blossom."

"She was your woman, was she?"

Longarm caught the "was" and took a deep breath. "Damn it, man!" he cried, looking back down at the cabin. "Where is she?"

"She's not down there. Not any more. She's up here."

Longarm felt a flood of relief. Blossom must have gotten away, then. "She all right?"

"I didn't say that. I spent all day yesterday building her a pine coffin."

Longarm felt as if he had been kicked in the stomach. In his mind's eye he saw Blossom standing near the door handing him the buckskin gloves she had made for him.

"Oh, Lord," he whispered.

"I could use some help with the coffin," Adams told him softly. Out of consideration for Longarm, he turned slightly and looked back at the stand of timber from which he had just emerged. "Can't bury it now. Snow's too deep and the ground's frozen. But I wanted to put it up in the trees, away from the wolves. In spring, I'll come back and bury it."

"Where is it?"

"Follow me."

A good half-mile from where Adams had stopped Longarm, they came to the spot where the trapper had fashioned a crude but solid coffin. About it lay the trapper's ax, handsaw, and adze. Longarm's first thought was how small the coffin was, and he tried to visualize Blossom. Had she really been that tiny. Then he was seeing her again as she entered the cabin that first morning, carrying the firewood, her dark cheeks aflame from the storm's wind.

"You found a suitable tree yet?" Longarm asked Adams.

Adams pointed to a large pine on the side of the steep slope. Its branches were spread out more than the usual pine. "That one should do."

Longarm nodded, and the two set to work. With the pine's snow-laden branches continually dumping snow on them, it was not an easy task lifting the coffin into the tree, then hauling it still higher until they had wedged it securely in the branches. At last, while Longarm held it steady, Adams lashed the coffin to the branches.

Longarm had not wanted to look inside it. He had no desire to see what the bastards had done to her. He preferred to remember her as he had last seen her.

Watching Adams pick up his tools, Longarm said, "What can you tell me, Adams?"

"You want to know how it was for her at the end?"

"Yes."

"It was her screams brought me to that ridge."

Longarm felt himself go numb. "Go on."

"I was checking some traps in a stream not far from here when I heard her. From the ridge I saw riders milling about in front of the cabin. Then two men dragged her out."

Adams paused, evidently reluctant to go on. Longarm waited.

"It was their leader—the tall Englishman—who finished your woman." Adams continued. "He was banged up some. I could see that even from the ridge. He had a bandage around his head, and he had another wrapped around his ribs. One arm was in a sling, his left. But he was able to ride and direct the bastards. Anyway, he was the one, sitting his horse, who questioned her last in front of the cabin. When she didn't tell him what he wanted to know, he shot her in the face."

"The bastard," Longarm said softly.

"Maybe yes. Maybe no. She wasn't wearing any clothes by that time, and there was not much skin left on her body."

After a moment Longarm asked, "You the one cut those two down?"

Adams nodded. "After the girl was killed, I lost my head some and started shooting. But I kept moving through the pines, picking off as many as I could. This Sharps has a long reach, and pretty soon they realized they were not fighting a woman any more. They lost heart and rode off."

"How many did you get? Just those two?"

"A couple of others, anyway. But I missed the bastard I really wanted."

"The leader?"

"Yes."

"I'm glad. I want him for myself."

"What's this all about, Barker? How come that bastard was after that woman?"

"He was after me, too. She was his housekeeper until she rode off with me. I took him as a hostage when I rode out. He escaped. That's why he looked so banged up. Thing is, when I had the chance, I should've finished him."

"Maybe so. Well, if you do take him, make it as slow as you can, hear?"

"I hear."

"You can't go back down to that cabin, Barker. I've seen it. It stinks of blood and death. Stay with me."

127

"You have a place around here?"

"Five miles up that stream I was trapping. It's a snug enough cabin, but there's enough room for one more."

Longarm explained about the sled and the haunch of horsemeat strapped to it.

Adams brightened. "I'll go with you. Fresh horsemeat can be very good, if it's cooked right. I have some rum to go with it. We'll have a feast and maybe forget that coffin up there for a while."

Not thinking of Blossom would be quite a trick if he could manage it. But this anger he felt was something he did not want to forget until the day he brought down John Masters.

Longarm thanked Adams for his offer of hospitality, then led the way down through the timber to where he had hidden the sled.

Chapter 11

That evening, sitting around a table Adams had constructed from old packing cases, the trapper told Longarm his odd history.

Born and brought up in Cambridge, Massachusetts, Franklin Adams was the son of a Harvard professor who was bound and determined to make a scholar of him. Close after his twenty-first birthday, however, it was discovered that Adams had contracted tuberculosis, and since both his younger sister and his older brother had perished from the same dread malady, young Adams decided he would go west to a more healthy climate in search of a cure, as so many others had done before him. When he found the West filling up with the same pestilential towns and cities he had fled in the East, he trekked north into the Canadian wilderness, and here at last he found a home.

That was ten years ago. As Longarm gazed upon Adams, he decided the man had indeed cured himself.

Never had he set eyes on anyone so obviously and so robustly healthy.

"You ever going back? To Massachusetts, I mean," asked Longarm.

"Death is waiting for me back there, Barker. Out here is life."

Adams got up then and led Longarm into a small room off the main room. It was no larger than a closet. An old army blanket served as a door. The high, narrow walls were lined with bookshelves. Crowding them were the works of Shakespeare, the novels of Sir Walter Scott, Thackeray, Dickens—and even a few by an American called Hawthorne. By far the largest number of books were by Dickens and Scott.

Every book appeared to be well-thumbed, Longarm noted, pulling down one book by Dickens. *Great Expectations,* it was called. He read a few of the opening paragraphs, then put the book on the shelf and returned to the main room with Adams.

"I reckon you turned out to be a scholar, after all," Longarm remarked, pulling his mug of rum closer. "Your father should be proud."

Adams nodded. "It's he who keeps me supplied. I journey to Toronto every spring for a new supply. He meets me there and we shop."

"He satisfied with you staying out here?"

"He understands perfectly. And every time he sees me, his eyes shine with pride. I guess he wishes he had thought of it for himself. He has not long to live. That loathsome disease now has its white fangs into him as well."

"And your mother?"

"She's gone, too."

"I see. I'm sorry, Adams."

There was a long silence after that. Longarm finished

the rum in his mug, then got up and went to the window. It was a bright night, moonlight spilling over the ghostly landscape, the wind howling softly in the pines about the place. Longarm found himself thinking of Blossom again.

And of John Masters.

The son of a bitch was sure as hell hard to kill. That fall from the ledge when Andrea cut the rope should have finished him. The only way Longarm could figure Masters's survival was that maybe the trees over which he was swinging had broken his fall enough to save him.

And now he was out after those who had done that to him.

Longarm turned to Adams. "Which direction did Masters and his men take when they rode off?"

"South."

"Toward Rock Lake?"

"That's right."

"How far is it from here?"

"Thirty miles, at least."

"If you can give me the loan of a horse, I'll be heading there first thing in the morning."

"Why?"

"It's a Meti stronghold, isn't it?"

"It is. I have many friends there," Adams replied.

"Would one of them be a fellow named Rene Dupre?"

"It would."

"Fine. A letter of introduction would do nicely."

"Why do you want to see him?"

"Let's just say he might be interested in the same thing I am," Longarm told him.

"And what might that be?"

"Stopping John Masters."

"Masters seems to be a hard man to stop. He looked pretty well banged up when I saw him last. But he was sure in control of those damned vigilantes. I must have thrown five or six rounds after him."

"Did you wing him, maybe?"

He shook his head. "I was too anxious."

Longarm left the window. "I better get some shuteye then. I'm leaving early."

"You won't need any letter of introduction, Barker."

"Why not?"

"I'm coming with you."

Two days later, a little before noon, Longarm and Adams rode into the town of Rock Lake. It looked as poor and cramped as Beaver Creek, jammed between a towering series of hills on one side and a mountain range on the other. The lake, frozen solidly now and covered with snow, sat in between the mountain and the hills, the town crowding its near shore.

As they rode down the muddy, snow-covered street, Adams let his horse drift close to Longarm's. "Something's wrong," Adams whispered. "The town is nearly deserted. And I don't see a single face I recognize."

The place did look pretty forlorn. There were horses and wagons pulled up to the hitch rails, but not too many. The few people Longarm saw on the walks seemed furtive, casting only sidelong glances at them as they rode past. Longarm glimpsed a barber watching from his shop. His barber chairs looked empty. They approached a large saloon. Here, at least, there was a large crowd of horses standing, their tails whisking impatiently in the cold air.

A sled broke from behind the livery stable, the dogs barking eagerly as they hit the traces. The driver, perched on the sled's runners, snapped his whip over their backs as he drove them out onto the frozen lake. Abruptly, from somewhere behind the livery, a rifle cracked, then another.

The sled's driver toppled forward into the snow. The sled kept on, the dogs still pulling eagerly. Longarm watched, but the sled's driver did not get up.

"What the hell?" Adams exclaimed incredulously.

Longarm was already reaching for his Colt when a familiar voice came from the sidewalk behind him. "Freeze, you bastard!" snapped Rance.

Longarm turned his head. Rance and two other men had their Colts trained on him and Adams. Behind them a familiar figure stepped out from a doorway: Masters. He looked a bit unsteady on his feet and he was covered with filthy bandages, but he was still able to heft a rifle.

The Metis must have ridden off somewhere, Longarm realized, allowing Masters and his mercenaries to ride in and take over the town. And now they were waiting for the Metis to return.

"Damn," said Adams bitterly. "It's a trap, and we rode right into it."

Longarm had no intention of suffering at the hands of Masters and his men, Rance especially. He yanked back on his horse's reins. The animal reared suddenly, his forelegs pawing wildly. By that time Longarm had his Colt out. He spurred the horse directly for Rance.

Rance cried out. There was a heavy thump as he was flattened by the charging horse. A shot roared from under it. Longarm felt the slug snick past his boot heel. Ignoring it, he drove the horse up onto the wooden sidewalk, heading straight for Masters. There was no time for Masters to haul up his rifle and fire. He leaped back into the doorway. Longarm reached over as he swept past and fired at the crouching Masters. The round went wild, shattering a huge plate-glass window. Longarm pulled the horse back onto the street and kept on going until he saw a line of Masters's

133

men completely blocking the street and his exit from the town.

He swung down a narrow, snow-filled alley. The horse found it heavy going and started to labor as it tried desperately to pull itself through the heavy drifts. Longarm leaped from the saddle, snaked his Winchester out of its scabbard, and dashed up a flight of back stairs to a landing.

He knocked once on the door, then pushed it open. He was in a kitchen. He ducked through it and found himself in a clean but meagerly furnished apartment. A man had been crouched by the window facing the front street. On Longarm's entrance, he jumped up and turned to face Longarm. There was a small, mean-looking hatchet clutched in his right hand.

Ignoring the hatchet, Longarm hurried past him to the window and looked down at the street. Adams was on his back in the snow, two men covering him. His fur cap was off and there appeared to be some blood on the side of his head. But he was alive and as Longarm watched, the two men hauled him upright and marched him across the street to the saloon.

Longarm went back to the door he had just come through, opened it a crack, and looked out. He was just in time to see a couple of riders, their horse struggling frantically in the snow, trying to catch up to Longarm's horse as it disappeared into an alley farther down.

He pulled the door shut and turned to face the fellow whose apartment he had just invaded. The man was tall and wiry, with a black bushy beard covering the lower portion of his face. He was frowning nervously as he looked Longarm up and down.

"My name's Pete Roulé," he said. "I'd invite you into my place formal-like, mister, but you don't seem to need an invite. Who the hell are you, anyway?"

"Never mind who I am," Longarm replied. "It don't look like you're working for Masters. That right?"

"Me work for that English Protestant son of a bitch!"

Longarm smiled. "And that's all either of us need to know. We're on the same side, at least for now."

"I saw them close in on you down there. You move fast, mister."

"Maybe so, but right now I need your help."

"If you want to help me, get the men left in this town weapons. Masters and his hired guns've taken most every shootin' iron in the place."

"Where are the rest of the townsmen? I saw precious few when I rode in."

"Them as stayed behind and got caught by Masters are in the saloon across the street. All of them. Masters is using it to corral them."

"He didn't get you, I see."

"And he didn't get a couple of others. We're keeping our tails down until it comes time to make our move."

"How the hell did Masters manage this?"

The man shrugged ruefully. "Him and his men rode in after dark a couple of nights ago. It didn't take them long to find out that most of the menfolk were gone. So they spread out and kept quiet until daybreak. Then they just marched around disarming everybody. Now they're waiting for Dupre and Roubison to get back with the rest of the men."

"Where are Dupre and Roubison off to?"

"They're retaking the mine."

"The Bonaventure?"

"That's right?"

"How many men did they take with them?"

"Better than fifty." He smiled grimly. "And when they

get back, they'll fix Masters's wagon. And I'll be joinin' them."

"They won't fix Masters if they aren't warned he's taken the town."

"That's all been taken care of. Gene LaBeau left on his dogsled just about the time you two showed up."

"Then you don't know."

"Know what?"

"LaBeau isn't going anywhere. One of Masters's men cut him down. He's lying out there now on the lake, and his dogsled's long gone."

"Jesus," he said. "I heard a shot, but I thought it was one of Masters's men warning you two to hold up." He shook his head, frowning. "LaBeau was a good man." Then he sighed and looked grimly up at Longarm. "Well, maybe that don't matter none. Dupre got more men than Masters. Soon's he sees the situation here, he'll move in and clean this town out, you'll see."

"It won't be that easy."

"Why not?"

"Where are the women? I didn't see any when I rode in. Are they still in town?"

"Sure. But they're keepin' inside, out of sight. Like we are. Masters's men already checked out this apartment. They think it's empty."

"But don't you figure Masters and his men know the women are here, even if they are keeping low?"

"Sure, they know."

"And when the time comes, Roulé, those women will make excellent hostages."

Roulé nodded unhappily. "So we send someone else to warn Dupre."

"Yes."

"But we already tried that."

"Try again. Dupre and Roubison have to warned, or they will ride in here and get taken as easily as me and my friend. And if they retake the town, they're going to have to do it with a night assault, and quickly, before Masters has a chance to use any of the women as hostages."

"Then maybe you better go, mister."

"I don't know where this mine is. You go."

"Not me."

"Why not?"

"The reason is standing behind you."

Longarm turned. A dark, very pretty woman with a red polka-dot kerchief over her head, dressed in a buckskin skirt and leggings, was standing in an open doorway leading from the bedroom. She had an old but well-oiled 12-gauge shotgun in her hand, and it was trained on Longarm.

"Oh," Longarm said.

"Meet my wife. Her name is Marie."

Longarm nodded politely, touching the brim of his hat. She offered no response, her coal-black eyes regarding him calmly. She looked more Indian than white, and she sure as hell moved quietly.

"I ain't leaving Marie to them bastards down there," Roulé told Longarm.

"You think if they discover her up here with you you'll be able to fight all of Masters's men off? Likely as not you'll end up killing yourself *and* your wife."

"Put the gun down, Marie," Roulé said to his wife.

"I think we should both go, Pete," Longarm told the man.

"I don't know you. You won't even tell me your name."

"You want a name? Try Barker. Ned Barker."

He shrugged. "That's good enough, I guess."

"You take that shotgun. How many shells you got for it?"

"Ten."

"Buckshot?"

"Double O."

"That should do nicely. One more thing. Has Masters been looking for anyone special?"

"Sure. Dupre's sister, Andrea. But she's hid good under the general store in a root cellar with my sister. She'll be safe there—if she don't try anything."

"You think she might?" Longarm asked.

"It's possible. She's just about as wild as her brother."

"You know her?"

"Yeah. I know her."

"Okay, when do we move out?"

"As soon as it gets dark." He looked over at his wife. "Get us some grub, will you, Marie? And pack something for us to take. We'll need it."

She started past him to the kitchen. Then she stopped in the doorway and turned around to face him. "I will pack enough for the three of us," she told him, in a voice that brooked no disagreement.

Roulé looked helplessly at Longarm and shrugged.

It was close to midnight, but the moonlight reflecting off the snow had nearly turned night back into day. Ahead of them, at the head of the alley, one of Masters's men was leaning wearily back against a building, smoking a cigarette. He showed no signs of tiring and kept glancing about him alertly. The three of them had been waiting now for at least ten minutes, hoping he would tire of staying in one place and move on. But this sentry was evidently determined to stay where he had been told to stay. Just beyond him was the frozen lake and the thick brush and timber that grew along its bank. Once the three of them reached that brush they would have cover.

138

"We'll have to kill the son of a bitch," said Pete finally, "or we'll be here all night."

"Let me do it," said Marie.

Longarm was startled. Before he could say anything, she moved silently past him and her husband. Ducking into the shadows along the wall, she vanished. Longarm squinted, looking for some sign of her, but it was as if she had vanished into thin air. He heard a soft sigh, like a horse makes sometimes when you lift off the saddle. The sentry vanished. A moment later Marie reappeared, beckoning to them.

With Pete leading the way, they reached the lake shore without further incident and set out through the brush. Their plan was to get out of sight of the town and then strike out across the frozen lake. It was the shortest way to the mine, Pete explained.

As they hurried along, Longarm asked Pete what his wife had used on that sentry.

"I didn't ask her and I ain't going to."

"You don't know?"

"I don't care."

They were in luck. An hour later they came upon LaBeau's dogsled and team. The dogs' traces were hopelessly tangled in the brush along the shore, and the dogs were whining pitifully, completely exhausted from their fruitless attempts to pull the sled free. Some of them had gnawed through their traces, but their shoulder harnesses still held them.

"You think we can untangle this mess?" Longarm asked.

"No problem," Pete said. "We'll just have to use fewer traces."

Even as he spoke, Marie was bent beside the dogs. Lips curling back to reveal their frustration, the dogs snapped ungratefully at the woman as she attempted to quiet them with soft words. Deftly she reached into the tangle and began unraveling the traces from around their legs and tails. Before long the dogs were silent, patiently willing for the girl to free them.

In less than half an hour the team was ready to go. LaBeau's whip had been found snared in the tangle. Snapping it judiciously over the dogs' heads, Pete drove the team across the lake, the sled cutting nicely through the snow. Bundled up snugly, Marie rode in the sled. Longarm trotted alongside, using the sled's right handle to help pull him along.

The pace was swift. Even though the snow was not as deep as what he had left behind in the mountains, it was tough going. As he panted alongside the sled, he thought longingly of the high, dry, rocking deck of a leather saddle.

Chapter 12

Close to sundown on the following day they saw the Metis column, on their way back from the mine, riding into the front yard of a rambling farmhouse in a snow-filled valley below them. The farmhouse stood out starkly against the solid white fields that surrounded it on all sides.

In their midst Longarm glimpsed several Mounted Police prisoners, their red tunics standing out against the snow. It seemed a jubilant band of Metis that rode their tough Indian ponies into the farmyard. The recapture of the Bonaventure mine had obviously been accomplished with a minimum of casualties, judging from the looks of it.

Pete directed the dogsled down the gentle slope toward the farmhouse. But the time the dogs pulled the sled into the yard, most of the Metis were crowded into the barns and the single bunkhouse. The dogs collapsed in their traces, exhausted, and Marie went to find food for them before they turned mean.

It was the two leaders Pete and Longarm wanted. Greeting a few of the Metis amiably, Pete led the way to the farmhouse door. He knocked and they were let in by a daughter of the house, who seemed delighted at all the excitement.

The two leaders were in the kitchen, sitting at a rough log table, while the Metis farmer and his wife were hastily stuffing wood into the stove. They had prodigious amounts of coffee yet to make and considerable amounts of food to feed the bellies of this small army. But from the look on their faces, it was a task they did not begrudge in the least.

As Longarm pulled up beside the table with Pete, he recognized at once the nearest Metis leader. He had seen him twice before—once when he burst into Longarm's hotel room in Moosehead, and a second time later that same night when he frantically poled his flat-bottomed boat across the Pembina River, leaving his men to their fate at the hands of Sheriff Bullock's smugglers. As he regarded Longarm, the tall lawman saw a gleam of recognition in the short, dark Meti's eyes. That description Andrea had sent to her brother had been a good one, all right. Even without his mustache, Longarm was recognizable.

The other Meti turned in his chair at their approach. Taller than his companion, his light beard and blue eyes were as untypical of the other Metis in appearance as was Longarm himself. But he dressed like them, and the cool arrogance in his eyes as he looked over Longarm and Pete was typical of the Metis. He was wearing a fur cap, a bright sash around his waist, and moccasins on his feet. Buckskin leggings protected his legs from the cold, and his vest, in typical Metis fashion, was buttoned only at the top.

It was he who spoke first. "What brings you and Marie out here, Pete?"

"We got trouble in town, Roubison," Pete replied. "Bad trouble."

"Protestant trouble?" demanded his companion.

Pete nodded. "That's right, Rene. John Masters has taken over the town."

"What in blazes!"

"And right now they're waiting for you to ride in. They figure they'll be able to cut you all down before you know what hit you."

"That would make him quite a hero in Ottawa," Dupre remarked grimly to Roubison, "after what we just done."

Roubison asked Pete for more details. When he got them, he took a deep, weary breath as he considered the implications of this unsettling news. Then he turned his attention to Longarm.

"Who are you, mister? I ain't seen you before, and you sure as hell ain't one of us."

Before Longarm could reply, Pete broke in hastily. "He's okay, Roubison. His name's Ned Barker. He's after Masters himself. He and Adams rode into town together. Before Masters could drop his loop over him, this one broke free?"

"That so?" Dupre grinned.

"And he trampled that segundo of Masters while he was at it."

"Rance?"

"Yep. Rance didn't look too good when they hauled him off."

Dupre lifted his Colt from his holster and laid it down carefully on the table in front of him. "Roubison," he said, grinning at Longarm, "meet the famous lawman from Denver, Custis Long."

"My friends call me Longarm."

Roubison was momentarily startled. Then he smiled

143

broadly up at Longarm. "Why, hell, Longarm, we been hearing all kinds of things about you. I hear Ottawa and your own government sent you up here to bring back Rene, here."

"And the silver certificates he robbed from a Wisconsin bank."

Pete was following this conversation with more than a little difficulty, glancing in amazement from Longarm back to Dupre. It was clear he had heard nothing about a lawman named Custis Long and knew even less about stolen silver certificates.

"So what are you doing out here?" demanded Rene Dupre coldly. "Why ain't you back in that town with Masters waiting to cut us down? You're on his side of the fence."

"I was when I hit Moosehead, Dupre. But not now."

"You got religion, did you?" said Roubison.

"Something like that—or I wouldn't be out here with Pete warning you of Masters, especially on foot, running behind a dogsled."

"That's right," said Pete, eager to repair the situation. "He's the one made me break out of town to warn you. Honest! When LaBeau tried to escape town, they shot him."

Roubison looked at Longarm with renewed interest. "Our cause is just, lawman. I guess you found that out once you got a closer look. That it?"

Longarm nodded. "Masters helped some in that regard."

Roubison smiled, pleased. "As I have said so often, a good cause is sometimes helped by the character of its opposition. Masters is a case in point."

"I don't trust this one," said Dupre.

"It is wise to trust no man," agreed Roubison, "completely. But I turn no man away if I can use him and I make

144

allies whenever possible. It was Lincoln who said the best way to get rid of enemies is to make friends of them. I agree. Ride with us, Longarm, but don't expect to take Dupre back with you. And forget about those silver certificates. I assure you, on my word of honor, we had nothing at all to do with that robbery."

Longarm made no effort to contradict the man. It was obvious he believed what he was saying—and, after all, he had nothing to hide. If he had been behind the robbing of that bank, he would have admitted it freely. Longarm decided he could trust Roubison.

But he had no such faith in Rene Dupre.

"My sister," Dupre said, addressing Pete. "Is she all right?"

"When I left she was," Pete told him. "She's in hiding, like the rest of the women."

Dupre turned to Roubison. "I say we hurry."

"I say we hold up and make plans first. If Masters has the town, he has a great advantage."

"But we know he's there."

"So that's *our* advantage. I suggest we not discard it by precipitate action."

"Do you mind if I suggest something?" Longarm said.

"Of course not. Let's hear what the U. S. marshal has to say."

"The men you left behind have been disarmed and herded into the saloon. They're in there now, waiting. Arm them. When you move on the town from outside, you would have help from within. Those men could see to the safety of the women while cutting down Masters's men."

"How would you get the arms to those men?"

"Pete and I. We could bring it in to them."

"At night."

"Yes."

"If either of you got caught by Masters or his men, you'd be dead men."

"We won't get caught." Longarm looked at Pete. "Will we, Pete?"

"Hell, no."

"I say it's too risky," said Dupre. "If they are discovered bringing in the guns, Masters will know we're nearby."

"He won't know any more than we tell him. We could just be arming the men for a break-out."

Roubison nodded quickly. "I like it. It has the virtue of simplicity, and if it works, we'll have that bastard Masters in a pincers. He won't know what hit him."

"Sure," said Pete nervously. "If it works."

With the Metis force waiting behind them in the timber along the lake, Longarm and Pete kept to the lake's shoreline as they pulled the dogsled closer to the town. The sled was heavy with weapons, both rifles and handguns. There was a full moon, but it kept passing in and out of the clouds. When it was behind a particularly large cloud, they would make a few hundred yards. When it shot out into the clear again, they would go flat and wait. It made for a long and uncomfortable two hours, but they were in no hurry. The frontal assault on the town would not take place until dawn. They still had another hour, at least.

Pete knew of a side entrance to the saloon, one used only when they had to bring in barrels for the bar. It was the first landing of the outside stairs, hidden behind a pile of discarded barrels. This made it unlikely there would be anyone guarding it. There were two of Masters's men at the head of the alley that led behind the saloon, however, and they showed no sign of moving away from their post.

"We'll have to take them," Longarm told Pete.

He nodded and moistened his lips. "You want me to do it?"

"No. Just stay here and watch."

Longarm darted across the narrow street to the side of the saloon, then ducked into the alley. Making no attempt to hide his presence, he walked directly up to the two sentries.

The two men straightened alertly at his approach. "Hey, mister," one of them said. "You better stop right there."

Longarm kept on walking. "Why?" he asked.

"Because I said so."

"I just came out to take a leak."

The other fellow laughed. "Why the hell didn't you say so?"

By that time Longarm had reached the closest one. With the barrel of his Colt, Longarm clubbed the sentry on the head with one single downward stroke. While the sentry sank to the ground, Longarm grabbed his companion about the throat, dragged him into the shadows, and clubbed him unconscious also.

A moment later, panting with the sudden exertion, Pete pulled the sled to a halt under the back stairs. Longarm found the door. He opened it as silently as he could and entered. He pushed through another narrow door and found himself behind the farthest corner of the bar. On the saloon floor the men were sprawled, resting or trying to sleep on blankets and pillows. A pot-bellied stove was thundering softly at the rear, sending waves of heat over the floor. The place stank. Near the saloon's entrance two of Masters's men were on guard. They both had shotguns. One was asleep in a chair; the other was staring out the window at the street.

Longarm looked around carefully to see if there were any other guards. Then he heard heavy boots on the balcony above the floor. Glancing up, he saw a guard toting a rifle, coming down the stairs. When he reached the floor, he told the guard in front of the window that he was going out back to take a leak.

Longarm ducked back outside. Pete had flattened against the wall, his Colt out, when he heard Longarm coming. Longarm darted past him and up onto the back porch. He was just in time. The rear door was pushed open and the guard strode through it. Longarm slugged him and then caught him about the shoulders and dragged him off the porch, then dumped him under it.

He hurried back to Pete then. "Start bringing them in. I'll pass them out. Be quiet. There's two guards still in there."

Longarm moved back into the saloon and waited behind the bar as Pete began bringing the rifles and handguns in to him. As soon as he had a good supply, he ducked low, moved under the folding counter, and nudged the nearest fellow. He stirred.

Longarm nudged him with a Colt and whispered, "Pass this to the next man."

The fellow was awake in an instant. He swiftly passed the gun to the fellow beside him and turned back to Longarm for the next one. In less than ten minutes, all the handguns they had brought with them had been given out. Then they started on the rifles. These were more difficult to handle quietly, which was why Longarm had kept them back.

In about half an hour, every man on the floor had been provided with a loaded weapon. Even so, the place was as still as death. At the tavern entrance, one guard was still sleeping; the other one was staring out the window.

Abruptly, the one at the window turned around. Then he

nudged his sleeping partner. "Where's Rolfe?" he wanted to know.

Watching from behind the bar, Longarm knew that Rolfe was probably the fellow Longarm had decked when he went out to relieve himself.

His companion shrugged blearily. "When'd he go out?"

"Ten minutes ago, maybe longer. I don't like it."

"What do you want me to do?"

"Go see what the hell is wrong with him."

The fellow protested, but his partner insisted. Wearily, the fellow got up from his chair and, stepping carefully over the bodies sprawled in his path, made his way carefully to the rear.

When he pushed the door open a moment later, Longarm was waiting with the same greeting he had given Rolfe. He moved back inside. It was almost dawn. Word had been passed to the armed men that the first crack of a rifle from outside the town in the direction of the lake would be the signal for them to rise up and smite those who had taken their town. In only a few minutes that signal would come.

The saloon's two large windows were pale with the first light of day when the distant crack of a rifle alerted the men. The fellow at the batwings immediately opened the door and stepped out onto the porch—thereby saving his life, as every man rose from the floor, a rifle or a Colt gleaming in his fist.

"Get out of here!" Longarm yelled at them. "Find a target, and do your best to protect the women!"

It was the only instruction they needed. With a whoop, the men stormed out of the saloon. A few moments later the dawn's pale light came alive with the crackle of gunfire. Longarm stepped out onto the porch with Pete.

"Where did you say Andrea was hiding?"

"The general store. In back. Follow me."

They raced down the street toward the store. Two of Masters's men had mounted up and were charging down the street toward them, firing at the men on the sidewalks. Longarm crouched down behind a porch post, sighted carefully on the nearest rider, and shot him out of his saddle. The second rider turned his mount down a narrow alley. As Longarm and Pete crossed in front of the alley, they glanced into it and saw the rider being pulled bodily from his horse by two of the men from the saloon.

At that moment, from both ends of the street, Roubison and Dupre, each leading his own contingent of riders, swept into town. They poured a steady fire at Masters's men, most of whom were shooting from windows and the roofs of porches and buildings.

The air was alive with the whine of bullets. Windows dissolved into fragments. Keeping their heads low, Longarm and Pete ducked down the alley running alongside the general store. They came out behind it and entered. The door to the root cellar led from a trapdoor in the pantry. Pete pulled up the door and scurried down the ladder, Longarm following close behind him. A lantern hanging from a rafter clipped him on the side of his head.

"Who's there?" cried a fearful woman's voice from a distant corner.

"Me," said Pete. "Pete Roulé."

"Pete, what's going on up there? I hear shooting."

"We're giving Masters a run for his money. And the rest of the men are back now from the mine. Together, we're takin' this town back. Just stay low until the bullets stop flying."

Longarm lit the lantern that had assaulted him and saw

four women and a little girl resting back against potato sacks all around him. There was no sign of Andrea.

"Where's Andrea?" Longarm asked.

"The bastard took her," said a woman under Longarm's elbow. She looked as sweet and innocent as milk-and-bread soup, but she was sure as hell angry.

"You mean Masters?"

"Yes."

"Where'd he take her?"

"How the hell would I know?"

Pete spoke up. "He's been living in the apartment over the barbershop, last I heard."

Longarm ducked back out of the root cellar.

Chapter 13

Longarm kicked through the door. Masters was at an open window, shooting down at the street. He turned and fired wildly at Longarm. Hurtling into the room, Longarm fired back. The windowpane above Masters shattered. Longarm spun and fired again as Masters raced from the place, then sent two more quick shots after him. But they were too quick. One round plowed into the wall by the door; the other bit a chunk out of the doorframe.

By the time Longarm reached the steps, Masters was gone. Longarm went back into the apartment and looked out the window. Men, firing as they moved, were moving slowly, relentlessly down the street, keeping themselves close to buildings or crowding into the heads of alleys. Two horses and their riders were sprawled on the ground, staining the snow with their blood. Two Metis stormed five of Masters's men who were forted up on a porch. It was over in seconds as the Metis took the porch, then stormed after the fleeing men into the building. Coming from all over, the rapid gunfire sounded like a Fourth of July celebration.

But Longarm saw no sign of Masters.

He turned from the window and started to search the rooms for Andrea. He found her in a small bedroom in back. He wished he hadn't. She was lying on her back on the bed, naked, her face no longer recognizable. Her rib cage was crushed and her shoulders and arms were purple from the beating she had taken.

He assumed Andrea was dead, and turned to leave the room. Her groan, low and barely audible, brought him back around, incredulous that she should still be alive. He moved to her side quickly and bent close.

Her eyes were open, and they showed a momentary spark of pleasure at the sight of him.

"You . . . not dead!"

"No," he replied softly. "Blossom came back for me."

". . . should have used a knife on Masters."

"He do this to you?" Longarm asked.

"Yes," she breathed.

"I'm sorry I didn't let you kill him," Longarm said.

"It . . . hurts, Longarm. Can you make it stop hurting?"

"You'll be all right. We're taking the town back. We'll get a doctor up here for you right away."

"No . . . please! Help me to die . . . !"

"I can't do that."

Suddenly a look of pure venom crossed her battered face as she stared past Longarm. Longarm turned and found himself looking into the muzzle of Rance's big Colt revolver. He looked in worse shape than Masters had. But, like Masters, it didn't seem to be slowing him down any. Leaning on a makeshift crutch, he was obviously in considerable pain as he balanced himself in the doorway and managed to keep his revolver trained on Longarm.

Rance smiled. "Am I glad I found you, you son of a bitch! Look what you done to me. My leg's all tore up."

"I wish I'd killed you."

Fury twisted Rance's face. He fired, but Longarm was already darting to one side. Bringing up his Colt, he fired in a single motion. The bullet shattered Rance's crutch. Rance clutched frantically at the doorframe for support as he slowly slid down it to the floor. Longarm fired at him again, but the hammer came down on an empty cylinder.

On the floor, Rance fired up at Longarm. The round snicked through the fabric of his right sleeve as he flung himself at Rance. The struggle was short as Longarm twisted Rance's revolver out of his hand and fired point-blank into his chest. Rance shuddered. A second later he lay still, his sightless eyes looking at a corner of the ceiling.

Longarm got to his feet and looked over at Andrea. A fresh dark smear of blood was seeping out from under her body. He hurried back to the bed. One of Rance's bullets had entered just under her heart and ranged clear up to her neck, where it exited. He closed her wide, staring eyes and left the room to find her brother.

It took less than an hour for them to drive Masters from the town. He and about eight of his riders escaped from town and were last seen riding northeast—toward Beaver Creek, more than likely.

But before the town could settle down and organize a force large enough to go after them, something had to be done about the Mounted Police the Metis had captured when they seized the Bonaventure Mine. The debate on the issue took place in the saloon, with the unhappy Mounties sitting on wooden chairs along one wall, their bound hands resting in their laps.

Roubison was in charge of the meeting. He stood behind the bar, with one of his lieutenants by his side. He opened the proceedings with the announcement that he was convinced their best course was to release the captives unharmed, even give them fresh horses and provisions to make it back to their Fort Garry headquarters.

A distraught Rene Dupre, just back from the hasty burial of his sister, was not so willing to be charitable. Standing well away from the bar to demonstrate the extent of his disagreement with Roubison, he was the spokesman for that faction pushing for a summary execution of the captives and immediately challenged Roubison's reasoning. His followers, a minority of the Metis present, but a solid, articulate group, agreed loudly with Dupre. Most of them, Pete Roulé explained, had suffered the loss of loved ones as the result of the government's actions. The only course of action that made any sense to them was a swift and just vengeance—a prompt hanging, so they could get after Masters.

It was clear to Longarm that if Roubison did not defuse the issue with few, if any, hurt feelings, his movement was on the brink of a split that could deal their cause a fatal blow.

Roubison seemed entirely aware of the stakes at issue. Up until this moment, the argument had been impassioned but courteous. Dupre, however, had just uttered an obscenity when one of Roubison's followers suggested that the Mounted Police returning to their headquarters carry with them a petition for Ottawa, one that set out clearly their grievances and that was signed by every Meti in the town.

"That's not very polite," Roubison chided Rene. "Pierre has a good point. We have taken the Bonaventure Mine back. And we have sent packing one of their champions in the area. We now have their attention, I would say." There was a general murmur of agreement to that. Roubison smiled. "It is time perhaps for us to state our demands again. And it would help if in the process we released, unharmed, these Mounted Police. I think a petition would gain for us the sympathy of all fair-minded Canadians."

"I doubt it!" Rene snorted.

"Think a moment. It would show that our determination has not wavered, and it would be an excellent way to demonstrate our solidarity."

"You think that matters to them?"

"Of course it does!"

"We are Metis! We stink in their nostrils."

"What is your alternative?"

"You know what it is!"

"I see. Kill these men here. Butcher them!"

"Yes! Such an action is one these bloodless English will understand. It is all they will *ever* understand!"

"It would only make matters worse."

"My God, Roubison, how much worse could it be?"

A murmur of agreement to that swept through the crowded saloon, and those standing with Rene nodded emphatically.

Roubison saw that he was losing the debate. For too long the Metis had suffered at the hands of Ottawa's cold indifference. When the new Canadian nation purchased these lands from the Hudson's Bay Company, it did so without consulting those who had lived on its land for generations. Like the Indians below the border, the Metis were about to see all that mattered to them stolen by greedy newcomers from the East.

These captured officers represented a target upon which

157

they could vent their fury and their frustration. The men wanted not only justice, but blood as well.

Longarm had been watching all this with great interest. As soon as the town had been retaken, Dupre made sure that every man there knew Longarm's identity and why he was in Canada. Denying that he had anything to do with robbing the bank in Wisconsin, Dupre wanted Longarm locked up or sent packing, insisting that he was working hand in glove with Ottawa to discredit the Metis.

At the same time, since Longarm had helped the Metis defeat Masters, and had even risked his life to do so, Roubison insisted that, despite Dupre's objections, Longarm and Adams should be allowed to move about the town without restraint.

Now, clearing his throat, Longarm left the corner where he had been standing with Adams and Pete Roulé. As he strode toward the bar, the saloon immediately quieted. Longarm's tall figure commanded attention. Every eye turned to gaze at him. From Dupre's followers, however, there was an angry mutter.

Roubison spoke up quickly. "Yes, Marshal Long. Do you have anything to add to this debate?"

"I have."

"Speak up, then."

"I'm not a Canadian," Longarm said, his voice carrying easily to every corner of the crowded room, "and I'm not a Meti. I speak as an outsider. And for that reason, what I say may have some value. I will leave it to you to decide that, one way or the other."

"Get on with it," snapped Dupre.

"I don't think you can fight the British Empire, but maybe you can make it budge a little. One side wants to punish the English and these redcoats here should pay the price. Then there are some of you who want to try reason one more time, who want to send Ottawa a petition. Why not do both? Make these men in their bright red tunics suffer a little, but don't kill them—just give them something to bring back to Ottawa, an indication that you are reasonable men and can be dealt with on that basis."

"You don't favor executing these men, Marshal?"

"If this were war, they would be your prisoners, and no civilized nation executes prisoners of war. Their uniforms show them to be officers of the government in Ottawa. In defending that mine, they were only doing their sworn duty, and for that they deserve credit, not contumely."

"Credit, hell!" sang out one of the men standing by Dupre. "They ain't deservin' of credit, no more than Masters and his cutthroats."

"I disagree. Masters and his band of gunslicks are not sworn agents of the government in Ottawa, like these Mounted Police. Masters and his men are no better than outlaws. They serve only their own greed. With such men we have already dealt summarily, and in that I have joined you. Sixteen dead gunmen are piled up in that alley behind the livery. One of them—Rance Santee—I put there myself. But these Mounties are not part of that."

"Then you would give them horses, set them free?" asked Roubison.

"Not entirely."

"What do you mean?"

"Why not let them walk back to their headquarters?"

"Walk?"

"You heard me," Longarm said.

"In this weather?"

"Some will make it, some won't. But give them a petition to take with them in any case. You will not have executed them outright, and those who survive will live to bring your message to the attention of Ottawa—indeed, all of Canada. Every newspaper in the province will cover the story."

"Suppose none of them make it?"

"In that case, your petition will not be needed to arouse Canada."

"Capital idea!" cried Roubison. He looked at Rene Dupre. "Both goals will be accomplished with one single stroke. What do you say, Rene? In this, at least, let us speak with a single voice."

Without giving Rene a chance to respond, he turned back to the crowded saloon. "Let's hear your voices, my friends! Is it to be the marshal's compromise?"

The men's affirmative response thundered through the saloon. Then came cheers at the break in the deadlock. Glancing over at the red-faced Dupre, Longarm saw him shrug his shoulders angrily. Dupre didn't like it, but the officers would be allowed to live.

Or at least they would survive as long as they could in as harsh and frigid an environment as Longarm could imagine.

As the saloon emptied, Longarm approached Roubison. "I'd like a chance to talk with you in private," Longarm told him. "You got the time?"

"Of course. Would my room at the hotel suit you?"

"That's okay with me."

"Seven o'clock this evening, then."

"I'll be there," said Longarm.

Roubison got up from his chair and strode over to the window, a troubled look on his face as he considered what Longarm had spent the past half-hour telling him. He stared out at the frozen lake for a long while, puffing on his cheroot. At length, he turned away from the window and

160

fixed Longarm with a hard, unhappy stare. Longarm was leaning back on the sofa, smoking a cheroot also.

"I don't want to believe you, Longarm."

"I know that."

"Rene Dupre's loyalty is the rock upon which I have counted these past three years. And his voice carries great weight in our councils. In addition to all that, there's really nothing in what you say that indicates he is not loyal to the Metis cause."

"Unless it be his dishonesty in not telling you what he has been doing: the smuggling, for one thing, and that bank robbery, for another."

"But what proof do you have that he *did* rob that bank in Wisconsin?"

"None."

Roubison shrugged. "You see?"

"Think a moment. Can you afford to have a man at your right hand who has stolen that much money—supposedly for the cause of Metis freedom—and yet has told you nothing about it? It seems pretty damn clear to me what he has been doing: using this Metis unrest to line his own pockets."

"That is a terrible charge."

"It explains why he went to such lengths to kill the man I was meeting in Moosehead, and why he made that attempt on my life later."

"You're positive it was him? The hotel room was dark, you said."

"And I was hanging from the roof. I know. But there's no doubt in my mind. It was Rene Dupre who charged into my room with those two others. And later, it was he who left his people behind at the Pembina River."

"When Sheriff Bullock was killed, you mean."

"Yes. And before he died, Bullock made it clear to me

what that ruckus was all about. He and Dupre were battling for the right to use the crossing for their smuggling operations."

Roubison shook his head. He was obviously finding it difficult to take all this in.

"I can understand how you must feel, Roubison. But this is what I've been able to piece together in the past weeks. Looking at all the evidence, it's the only explanation that makes sense."

"Perhaps I should not be so surprised. I must admit, it would explain much."

"How so?"

"Rene has been increasingly difficult to handle of late. He goes his own way, and lately I've noticed he seems to have resources greater than mine. His people are better armed than mine, and more and more of the men are listening to his call for violence—for all-out war. These adventures of his would be perfectly in keeping with his penchant for action, and his often reckless disregard for the consequences."

"Sometimes outlaws find a real home in movements like yours. It gives them an excuse to do what they would not dare contemplate otherwise."

"Like robbing banks in Wisconsin?"

"Or smuggling rum into Canada to trade with the Indians. Or killing anyone who might threaten their success," Longarm said.

"I still find it difficult to believe."

"But not impossible?"

"No. Sadly, not impossible," Roubison admitted.

"As you said, I have no proof. But if I could get hold of a few of those silver certificates—find them in Dupre's possession, say—that would nail it down for me."

"And for me, as well."

"Does he have a cabin nearby?" Longarm asked.

"Not nearby. About twenty-five miles from here, along Pellican Lake. He spends winters in town here, but as soon as spring comes, he moves back out there."

"How can I leave here without arousing suspicion? I'm certain Dupre will be keeping pretty close watch on me, though I doubt if he'll try what he did in Moosehead."

Roubison thought for a moment. "Suppose I manage it for you and your friend to escort the Mounted Police out of town? You don't have to come right back, of course."

"Yes. That might do it."

"I'll see to it. Since it was your idea to set the poor bastards loose on foot anyway, it won't seem at all out of order for you to give them their marching orders and start them on their way. I suggest you be ready to ride out first thing in the morning."

Longarm got to his feet and the two men shook on it.

The Mounties were still in sight. For almost an eternity, it seemed, they had been moving across the distant flat. So far were they that the color of their tunics was no longer visible. They looked to Longarm like a column of ants struggling across an immense white tablecloth.

He glanced up at the sky. It was still clear and blue. The wind coming from the northwest was cold. It cut against his cheekbones like a razor. He had regrown his mustache and he liked to imagine that this additional hair prevented his upper lip from freezing solid and dropping off.

"Let's go," Longarm said, turning his horse south to Pellican Lake.

"You sure Dupre has no idea what we're up to?" Adams asked, slapping his mittened hands together to warm them up.

"I'm not sure of anything, except that the best way to keep warm is to keep moving."

It was past sundown when they reached the cabin on Pelican Lake. By that time the temperature must have dropped to twenty below. Longarm thought of those Mounties struggling through the frigid night and shuddered in sympathy.

Riding into the yard of Dupre's cabin, they dismounted and led their mounts into the small barn beside the cabin. The four stalls were empty, but there was plenty of hay about, and after a little searching, Adams came up with half a sack of grain and some wooden buckets. There was no water, so Longarm packed snow into two of the buckets and placed one inside each stall, expecting the heat of the animals' bodies to melt the snow eventually.

They had little difficulty getting into the cabin. Lighting the lamps they found, they built a fire in the fireplace, then began their hunt for the silver certificates. For more than an hour, they searched every possible hiding place, but they found nothing. They were about to give up when Longarm noticed an irregularity in the boards a few feet to one side of the fireplace, as if they had been cut through at that spot, then folded back.

"Over there!" Longarm said.

They discovered a loose piece of flooring alongside the crack, lifted it out, and found a handle. Hauling up on it, they found themselves lifting a trapdoor that revealed a hidden passageway. A wooden ladder led straight down. Taking a lantern, Longarm climbed down first. Adams followed. The passageway led to a heavy door. It was not locked. They pulled open the door and stepped into a large storeroom.

Adams uttered a long, low whistle as Longarm held the lantern high and slowly brought it around.

"There's enough in here to start a war," Adams said.

"To start and win one."

Rifles were stacked against the walls, along with boxes of dynamite, coils of Bickford fuses, and barrels of gunpowder. In the far corner they found two Gatling guns, not yet completely assembled, and boxes of cartridges piled clear to the ceiling, enough rounds to keep an army going for weeks.

They searched for the money everywhere: on the shelves, in the corners, in the rafters. They peered behind every rifle, handgun, and box. Then they emptied the boxes and felt around inside them. The lantern ran out of oil, and they refilled it and continued their search. It took at least two hours for them to cover every inch of the storeroom and the passageway leading into it. They even probed the earthen walls with a crowbar they found, hoping to find a hidden chamber.

They found no money at all. Looking at the weapons cache, Longarm wondered if this was where the money had gone. They climbed back out of the passageway and, somewhat discouraged, dropped the trapdoor back into place. Undaunted, they tried the barn next, searching the loft, walls, storage closets, and shelves. Again, they found nothing.

Frozen half to death, they returned to the cabin.

"We're looking for a needle in a haystack," said Adams, "if you'll excuse me for being so original."

"And we're not really sure the needle was placed in this particular haystack to begin with. Still, Dupre couldn't just carry the money around with him."

"Maybe he has already spent it on that arsenal below us."

"Could be. But how could he cash those certificates, then buy all that weaponry, without causing a stir? As soon as he went to any banks up here to exchange the certificates for Canadian currency, he would be giving himself away. He must know that."

"Then why steal this money in the first place?" Adams wondered.

"Maybe it's mad money."

"What?"

"In case things go bad up here, he can ride south and spend the money at his leisure," Longarm explained. "He could live the rest of his life like a king. Louis Riel is a Metis leader in exile right now in Montana, but he's not living so well, and maybe that's what Dupre is getting himself ready for—a comfortable exile."

Longarm suddenly wiped at his eyes. They were stinging painfully. He glanced toward the fireplace and saw that the fire was close to going out, and the smoke was pulsing back into the room.

Adams was squinting also. "Something's wrong with that fireplace," he said, starting toward it. "I opened the damper as wide as possible, but it ain't drawing worth a damn."

By the time they reached the fireplace, the fire was so low they were able to stomp it out with their boots. Meanwhile, the room had become filled up with smoke. They were forced to open both the front and back doors to clear the air.

Once the smoke had cleared out—and this did not take long as the frigid wind howled through the cabin—Longarm, holding the lantern just right, craned his neck so he could look up into the chimney. A few feet above the damper, something was wedged across the flue.

"I can't make out what it is exactly, but it looks like a

short piece of charred wood," Longarm said, pulling his head out of the chimney. "Maybe a beam of some kind."

"Let me see if I can get it out," Adams said.

As Adams reached up past the damper, Longarm held the lantern so he could see. After a few muttered curses, Adams managed to grab hold of the obstruction and pull it out.

Only it wasn't a beam or a piece of charred wood.

It was a steel cash box.

Chapter 14

The box was blackened by the fire and still hot to the touch. Adams put it down on the table. There was a small padlock, which Longarm shattered with a single shot from his .44. Lifting its lid, they found not only the silver certificates, but sacks of double eagles.

"Yep. No question, I guess," said Adams. "This here's an insurance policy, in case things get too hot up here and the Canadian authorities pull out all the stops."

"And it's proof positive," said Longarm. "Roubison will have no reason not to hand Dupre over to me now."

"Even so, I doubt if he'll do it, Longarm."

"Reckon you're right, at that. I been thinking the same thing myself. But this here loot is strong evidence."

"What's that?" Adams said suddenly.

Longarm had heard it, too: the chink of distant bits, then the blowing of a horse, maybe two horses. Longarm closed the box, then led Adams out the back door and around to the side of the house.

Crouching in a snow bank, they peered past the front yard and saw the line of riders approaching through the night. They were clear enough in the moonlight reflected off the snow. Longarm counted eight riders in all. He had no trouble recognizing the lead rider, since he was so thoroughly bandaged.

It was John Masters.

"Get back inside," Longarm told Adams.

As soon as they were inside the cabin, Longarm pulled up the trapdoor. "Take my rifle," he told Adams. "Run straight out the back door. Leave it open. Pull up when you find cover. They'll think we both ran out that way. Open up on them as soon as they clear the cabin, and drive them back into it."

"What are you going to do?"

Longarm started down the ladder. "I'll just pop up like a jack in the box and surprise the hell out of them."

"Good luck, Longarm," Adams said, grinning.

He snatched up Longarm's rifle and bolted out the back door, being sure to leave it wide open.

Longarm blew out the lantern and closed the trapdoor over his head. Then he waited. Crouching in the darkness, listening for the tramp of running boots, he asked himself what in blazes Masters was doing here.

No sooner did he pose the question than he knew the answer. Like them, but for entirely different reasons, Masters had come for the money. Before Masters had beaten Andrea nearly to death, she must have told Masters where her brother had hidden the money he and his gang had stolen from the Wisconsin bank. Longarm remembered how easily Andrea had admitted knowledge of the silver certificates. Apparently she had also known where her brother had put them.

The front door was suddenly flung open. A flurry of heavy boots pounded on the floor above him. Someone saw the open door, shouted something, and the men ran across the cabin floor and out through the open doorway into the night. Dim shouts came to Longarm then as the men plunged through the snow, following Adams's tracks. The distant bark of Longarm's Winchester came suddenly. There was answering fire, followed by the sound of men crying out. Adams was a good shot, evidently, even by the light of the moon.

At once the floor above Longarm reverberated with the pounding of running feet as Masters and his men retreated into the cabin. Ramming upward with his head and shoulder, Longarm slammed the trapdoor open and steadied himself on the second rung of the ladder.

Looking at him in amazement, the two closest men began firing wildly at him. Carefully, Longarm returned their fire. Both men toppled to the floor.

Masters was near the doorway. "Cut the bastard down!" he cried to his men.

But Longarm was doing the shearing. One more, then another, fell before his withering fire. Masters's men had difficulty getting a clean shot at Longarm. They pushed frantically against each other in the cabin's narrow confines. The cabin's interior seemed to pulse with ear-shattering detonations. Firing up into the milling gunmen, Longarm heard their cries as his bullets tore into them. Acrid, blinding gunsmoke filled the place.

All of a sudden there was only Masters. Darting back outside the cabin, he fired in at Longarm. The slug punched a hole in the floor, showering Longarm with shards of wood. The sudden crack of a rifle came from just

171

outside the cabin. Masters cried out and staggered into the cabin. He was still armed and still dangerous. Longarm fired at him, this time deliberately aiming low.

Gutshot, Masters slammed sideways onto the floor, clutching at his stomach. He was in a mad terror, for he knew the kind of death he had bought with this wound.

His rifle at the ready, Adams poked his head cautiously into the cabin. "There's two men down out here," he told Longarm quickly. "They're hurt bad."

"We got more than that in here," Longarm replied, climbing up out of the passageway.

"Jesus," said Adams, as he stepped into the cabin. "I guess so."

The wounded men were twisting in pain on the floor. Longarm kicked their weapons into a far corner as he picked his way among them. One or two, he was afraid, would not be riding anywhere ever again.

He reached Masters and went down on one knee beside him.

Masters's face was green. Whether it was sheer terror at the thought of death, or the terrible pain, Longarm could not be sure. Whatever it was, the man was suffering.

"You're a dead man, Masters," Longarm told him.

"You bastard," Masters snarled, his voice weak from pain. "How'd you know I was comin' here?"

"I didn't. I came for the same reason you did—for the money."

"Andrea told you?"

"Nope. I just figured it had to be out here."

"You won't find it. You'll never find where Dupre hid it."

"I found it, Masters."

"If there's a hell, Longarm, we'll meet again."

"We will then. And I'll get to finish what I started here."

Masters tried to respond. Instead he gasped. "Oh, Jesus," Masters cried, his voice an ugly rasp. "It hurts!"

There was nothing Longarm could do for him. Nothing he wanted to do for him. He stood up and stepped back. He had thought he would be happy to see Masters suffering as he had made so many others suffer, but he wasn't.

He was just grimly satisfied to see justice done.

Within sight of Rock Lake, Adams said goodbye to Longarm and promised that, come spring, he would see to a proper burial for Blossom. Longarm sat his horse a while, watching Adams ride off. The man turned once and waved to him. Longarm waved back, then continued on to Rock Lake.

Dusk was falling as he rode into town. At sight of him there was an immediate reaction, men waving to him or running to tell others of his return. Before Longarm dismounted in front of Roubison's hotel, the Metis leader was waiting for him on the small porch. Longarm had transferred the stolen banknotes to his saddlebag and he lugged it with him when he entered the hotel.

Roubison ushered Longarm into his room and closed the door, telling the lawman how pleased he was to see him again. Longarm sat down in the sofa and draped his saddlebag over its arm.

"I see by the heft of that saddlebag," Roubison said, "that you did not return empty-handed."

"I did not."

"The stolen money was at Dupre's place?"

"It was."

Roubison sighed. "I was afraid of that."

"Where's Rene Dupre?" Longarm asked.

173

"There's no hurry, Longarm." He went over to a cabinet and poured two glasses of whiskey, then handed one to Longarm. "A toast."

Taking the whiskey, Longarm asked, "To what?"

"To the eventual success of the Metis over their oppressors in Ottawa."

With a casual shrug, Longarm drank to that. The fiery liquid warmed him instantly. It had been a long, cold ride from Dupre's place.

"Masters is dead," Longarm told Roubison.

"Are you sure?"

"He's dead, all right, along with a couple of his followers. The rest, wounded, I let go. They weren't in any condition to trouble you or your men any more."

"This is good news, Longarm! How did you manage it?"

Longarm explained briefly why he thought Masters and his men had shown up at Dupre's cabin, and how he and Adams had disposed of them. When he finished his account, Roubison shook his head worriedly.

"Well, this is going to be just one more excuse for Ottawa to increase their pressure on us, I am afraid. But it is worth it to see that man gone!"

"I wouldn't worry about it, Roubison. I don't think the death of John Masters is going to cause much of an uproar."

"Why do you say that?"

"There was quite an arsenal under Dupre's cabin. After we let his wounded men ride off, we dumped Masters and his two dead gunslicks into it, then set off the dynamite we found in Dupre's arsenal. It made a pretty good explosion. When the smoke cleared, there was not much left of Dupre's cabin, and even less of Masters and his men."

"Then Masters has simply disappeared."

"Without a trace."

"That will help some," Roubison agreed. "But this arsenal of Dupre's—how extensive was it?"

"Enough to equip a large force. A *very* large force," Longarm told him.

"I knew nothing of it."

"I didn't think you did."

"Then Rene has indeed been planning to break away from the rest of us."

"Yes. And, if that failed, he had this money here, to live pretty well in exile."

"Unlike Louis. Riel. He's in exile in Montana, you know."

"I know."

"Too bad you blew up all those weapons. We could use a bit more firepower if we are going to hold on to the mine."

"I had the wounded men transfer the bulk of the weapons and ammunition to the barn," Longarm told him. "It is there now, waiting for your men to collect it."

Roubison's eyes lit in appreciation. "You have done well, Longarm! I congratulate you."

"Thank you. Now, I want Rene Dupre. I won't try to get those who rode with him when he robbed the bank, but Dupre I want. I've dealt with you fairly. I expect the same from you."

Roubison did not reply immediately. With a heavy sigh, he went back to the liquor cabinet to freshen his drink. When he turned back around, there was a revolver in his hand instead of a glass. He cocked it.

"I am sorry, my friend," he said. "But I am afraid it would be impossible for me to turn Rene Dupre over to you. If my men were to see me do such a thing, I would be finished as their leader. I simply cannot allow it."

"This is not very fair, Roubison."

"Have you not heard that all things are fair in love and war?"

"This is neither."

"Believe me, Longarm, I have no choice."

There was a sudden pounding on the door. Still covering Longarm, Roubison crossed the room and opened the door a crack. "I am not to be disturbed!" he hissed.

But the man on the other side of the door spoke anyway, in French, and in a voice alive with excitement. Roubison exclaimed in astonishment, then closed the door.

"What is it?" Longarm asked.

"We are both in luck, my friend!" Roubison told him, his eyes alight. "Curfew shall not ring tonight!"

"I'm reprieved?"

"Yes!"

"Then put down that gun," Longarm said. "What happened?"

"Rene Dupre has fled. In one stroke he has rid me of a very difficult problem. Men loyal to me were holding him in a house not far from town. I guess when he heard you had ridden in with heavy saddlebags, he realized the game was up. What he did not know, of course, was that under no circumstances would I have turned him over to you."

"Ironic."

"Yes. He thought I was cut from his mold, I am afraid. Now he is out there on his own, no longer a part of our struggle."

"I guess that settles things."

"You are not going to track him down?" Roubison asked.

"It will be dark soon. He knows this country, and I

176

don't. Besides, where would I look? This is a big country. It's enough that I have the money he stole. Rene Dupre is out of action now, in a kind of exile, I suppose. That will be punishment enough, I should think."

"It will, believe me, Longarm. We Metis are a tough people, but we need each other. Outcasts in an alien world, we have no life apart from our own kind."

"I'll have another drink now," Longarm said. "And do you have any more of those cheroots?"

"I will light one for you myself!" Roubison told him as he poured Longarm a fresh libation.

Longarm rode into Crystal City a week later, around midnight, and left Roubison's chestnut in the livery. He took a room at the hotel, signing the register as Ned Barker. He had left this place with Sharon's brother Justin. He was returning without him, and he felt an obligation to find Sharon to explain to her and Tim about their brother's death. He would try to offer what consolation he could before continuing on to the North Dakota border. It was an unpleasant task he had set himself, and he was not looking forward to it.

The next morning he inquired at the livery stable and was given directions to Justin's small farmhouse. Curious stares followed him as he rode out. The townspeople remembered him, all right, and undoubtedly recalled as well why Justin had ridden off with him to Rock Lake.

But no one hailed him or tried to stop him, and soon enough Longarm had put the town behind him. He came to a stream that was frozen over and followed it for a couple of miles until he came to a wooded stretch punctuated with boulders and ravines. The going here was tough, with many deep snowdrifts that had to be negotiated carefully. At times Longarm was forced to dismount and lead his horse. He kept on through the timber and once he had put it behind him, he could see across a long flat. On the far edge of it, tucked cozily into one of the stream's sweeping meanders, was the small farmhouse Justin had built. There were several barns on the place, as well as chicken coops and shed. A thick plume of smoke coiled out of the chimney.

It took a surprisingly long while for him to cross the flat. The sun glancing off the snow kept him squinting all the way. When he reached the front yard of the farmhouse, he relaxed some—and then found himself suddenly wary.

By this time, someone should have come from the house to greet him. He pulled up abruptly. The horse gave his head a shake, jingling his bit. Longarm patted the chestnut's neck to settle him down. He could hear the chickens in the coop off to the right of the house. Smoke was still coming from the chimney.

He shrugged. He was being silly. Sharon was probably so busy baking bread or something that she had not taken even a moment to glance out the window. He urged the horse on again, heading for the front porch.

Something inside the house crashed violently to the floor. Then came the sound of glass breaking. The front door burst open and Tim ran out. He took the porch steps two at a time as he raced through the snow toward Longarm.

"He's in there!" Tim cried. "He's got Sharon!"

Longarm was already off his horse, snaking his Winchester from the boot. He slapped the chestnut smartly on the rump to send him plunging off toward the barn. Tim reached him then, slamming into him, his face dark with fear.

"Don't let him hurt Sharon! He said he would if we didn't keep quiet while you came in!"

"Who're you talking about?" Longarm asked the boy.

"Rene Dupre!"

Inside, Sharon screamed. Then came the muffled roar of a rifle. Longarm left Tim behind as his long legs took him up onto the porch and into the house. He glimpsed the back of Dupre's coat as he flung himself out the kitchen door. Longarm fired once, disintegrating a kitchen window, then held up. Before him on the kitchen floor lay Sharon. She had a neck wound, with blood flowing from it.

Longarm put his rifle aside and bent beside her. A quick examination showed the wound to be superficial, but the bleeding had to be stopped. Behind him, Tim gasped.

"Get some water on the stove. Heat it up. And get some clean linen I can use for bandaging her neck."

"Will . . . Is she . . ."

"She's going to be fine, Tim. Do as I say!"

At that moment Longarm heard the muffled thud of hoofs. He jumped up and glanced out the kitchen window. Dupre was riding a big black saddle horse across the flat toward the timber.

He went back to Sharon. Her eyes were open now. "I'll be all right," she said, trying to sit up.

"You're bleeding bad."

"It's just a flesh wound," she told him as she felt it. "Help me over to that chair by the table."

He did so and in a moment she was directing Tim as the boy poked more wood into the stove and set a kettle of water down onto it. She wrapped a towel about her neck and glanced up at Longarm.

"You see? I'm fine."

"What happened?"

"Rene intended to wait until you entered the kitchen. Then he was going to cut you down."

"As simple as that?"

"As simple and as terrible as that. When Justin and Dupre's sister were courting, I saw a lot of Dupre, too. I was as polite to him as I could be—for Justin's sake. But I could never abide the man. He was too violent, too extreme."

"That's him, all right."

"I'm glad to see you alive," she said with sudden warmth.

"Thanks to you, I still am. I'm going after him."

"Be careful."

Longarm snatched up his rifle.

Chapter 15

Longarm found the chestnut in the back of the barn, looking for a stall and swishing its tail nervously. Mounting up,
Longarm turned the horse, ducked low, and clattered out of
the barn. Dupre was still in sight, not yet halfway across
the flat.

Longarm spurred his mount after him. He closed on the
man swiftly, but before he could overtake him, Dupre vanished into the timber. A moment later Longarm reached the
rough, timbered area. Dupre's tracks were easy enough to
follow and Longarm noticed that the fleeing man was not
slowing his horse any, despite the treacherous terrain.

Longarm was not surprised when he saw Dupre's horse
thrashing feebly in a snow bank just beyond a small clearing ahead of him. He leaped from his horse, his Winchester in his hand. Ducking low, he headed for a pile of rocks
off to his left. Dupre appeared on the topmost rock, aimed,
and fired. Longarm had already flung himself aside, and

the shot went wild. Swiftly circling around behind the rocks, he started to climb them and heard Dupre scrambling down the other side. Longarm kept on, poked through a clump of juniper, and saw Dupre heading out onto the frozen stream that wound past the timber. He was heading for another stretch of timber on the far side. He never made it.

The swift water had not yet allowed the ice to thicken, and he plunged through. His cry was instant and terrified as he began thrashing back toward the more solid ice. Longarm raced out onto the ice and kept going until he felt it cracking ominously under him. He lay down flat and poked his rifle toward Dupre, stretching as far as he could. Frantically, Dupre grabbed at the rifle barrel. But each time he caught hold of it, his fingers, numbed by the frigid waters by this time, were unable to hang on.

He cried out in terror as he felt the strong current pulling him under the black water. Longarm saw his head vanish. It popped up a moment later. Dupre's mouth was open as he gasped for air. The current pulled him farther along until his head cracked against the edge of the ice. He was pulled under then and vanished.

Longarm pushed himself backward until he was sure of the ice. He stood up and looked at the dark hole, the swift water smooth as it swept along. Dupre did not reappear.

Shaken, Longarm turned and trudged back onto the shore. There had been something very terrible about Dupre's death. He could imagine the man, still alive, still struggling, trapped under the ice, the cold fist of death closing inexorably around him.

He had not expected to bring Rene Dupre back to stand trial. But he had not expected this, either.

* * *

"It's snowing again," he said, looking out at the quiet night. He was naked except for the bottom part of his longjohns.

"Yes."

Sharon was propped up on a pillow, her neck efficiently bandaged. Color was returning to her cheeks already. The bullet had narrowly missed her jugular, it turned out. An inch more and she would not be alive. Questioning Tim, Longarm found out that she had been standing close by the window with Dupre, the rifle tucked under her chin, his finger resting on the trigger. Any false move from her and she would be a dead woman.

Nevertheless, the moment she saw Longarm pull his horse to a halt, she had twisted away from Dupre and told Tim to run out the front door to warn him. While Tim did this, she had battled with Dupre for possession of the rifle.

It was during this struggle that the rifle had gone off.

He left the window and sat down on the edge of the bed. Taking her hand in his, he said, "You are a very brave woman."

"Don't forget Tim."

He smiled. "I won't."

He had already told her about her brother, and also who he was and why he was in Canada. But she had learned about her brother's death from Dupre a full week before, and it was no longer the shock it had been then. Learning Longarm's real identity seemed to make no difference to her. She was just glad to see him.

"Will you be leaving soon . . . I mean, for the States."

Longarm looked back toward the window. "That looks like a pretty big snow, doesn't it?"

She brightened mischievously. "It certainly does."

"Travel in this kind of weather can be dangerous."

"Foolhardy."

"I'll probably have to wait a while. A week, maybe more."

"I think that would be very sensible."

"The bank's waited this long for its money. It can wait a little longer."

"They won't even miss it."

He smiled, then bent over and kissed her gently on the lips. She reached up with her hand and pressed his head closer, opening her mouth to the pressure of his lips. When he pulled back finally, she smiled.

"You see? I feel much better."

"I'm glad."

"But it wouldn't be very kind of you to leave until I was fully recovered. Isn't that so?"

He blew out the lantern on the nightstand, then lifted the covers and slipped into the bed beside her. Resting his head on her warm breasts, he held her gently in his arms.

"Yes," he said. "That is so."

She laughed softly, kissed him lightly on the forehead, then promptly fell asleep. Longarm looked over at the window. The wind was rising, carrying gusts of snow with it. He could hear the snow striking the windowpanes. It was a comforting sound. For only a brief moment he thought of Billy Vail and the crowded, smoke-filled rooms of Denver.

Then he closed his eyes and slept.

Watch for

LONGARM AND THE ESCAPE ARTIST

ninety-fifth novel in the bold
LONGARM series from Jove

coming in November!

Explore the exciting Old West with
one of the men who made it wild!